THE BRIDESMAID AND HER SURPRISE LOVE

Wedding Games: Book Three

KAYLA TIRRELL

DAPHNE JAMES HUFF

ONE

4 Days Until Dream Wedding

MILO SLAPPED another mosquito off of his forearm.

"Dang mozzies."

He wasn't sure how long he was supposed to be hiding in the woods, but the skeezy producer had told him he'd be back when the time was right. Milo just hoped the time was soon. After a sixteen-hour plane ride, an hour car ride to the inn where his sister was filming this ridiculous reality show, and sitting behind the bushes in the middle of the woods for the last forty-five minutes, Milo was ready to be reunited with the rest of his family.

Only Audrey and Mom knew he was here, and those two reunions had been sweeter than he'd ever hoped for. He couldn't wait to see the joy on everyone else's faces when they realized he was home after ten years.

It had been a *long* ten years.

While he waited, he tried to enjoy the familiar scent of pine trees, and he watched a few fireflies in the distance, but even the comforting sights and smells of Wellspring weren't enough to calm the rapid beating of his heart. The yearning to see his other sisters wasn't a desire anymore, it was a need. He was so close, but he wouldn't be able to relax until he knew it was real—that he was finally home.

Milo's ears perked up at the sound of yelling closer to the barn, and even though Bruce Bigg had explicitly told Milo not to move from this spot, he crept closer to the voices. It was the all-too-familiar sound of a couple fighting.

He peered through the darkness, relying on the light from the scattered lamps to avoid stepping on a small branch or twig that would give away his presence. When the couple came into view, Milo recognized the girl.

It was Audrey. But that wasn't Eli she was with.

Milo's mind raced with possibilities. This was a reality show, after all. Was he a jilted ex? A secret lover?

Milo shook his head to clear the thought. Just because Kylie had manipulated him, didn't mean every female was constantly lying behind their loved one's back.

Then again, he hadn't seen Audrey in ten years, and the only reason he was able to now was because of the reality show. How much did he really know his sisters?

The only way to figure out what was going on was to get closer. He took a few more soft steps toward them, trying to listen, but it was no use. They'd stopped talking, and another girl had shown up.

Fair skin, blond hair. Another one of his sisters? He hated that he couldn't tell if it was Harper or Sienna, but they'd both been teenagers the last time he'd seen them. Whichever sister this was, it didn't matter. Just knowing he was a couple of feet away brought a small smile to his face.

But then Audrey walked off toward the inn, and the mystery guy and one of his sisters were left alone. In the middle of the woods.

What have you gotten everyone into, Audrey?

Milo strained his ears to hear the new conversation, but they were speaking more softly. With stealth he was unaware he possessed, he took a few more steps in their direction but was still unable to hear what they were saying. The only words he could make out were "idiot" and "getting in the way of my dreams." Milo's heart was suddenly racing.

It could have been nothing, but then why talk out here instead of in the inn? Milo tried to be reasonable and take into account how tired he was. Maybe he hadn't heard them properly. Besides, this guy looked decent enough, maybe he was just a friend, helping his sister during what was probably a stressful week. Milo sighed and leaned back against a tree trunk, the bark scratching his neck.

Guess I'll just have to be patient.

But then the mystery guy did something completely unforgivable.

He kissed Milo's little sister.

That was more than Milo could handle. He barged into the clearing just in time for the two to break apart. The guy started to say something, but Milo's heartbeat was pounding too loudly in his ears to hear it. He pulled back his arm, then punched the guy right in the face. There was an enormously satisfying crunching sound before the jerk fell to the ground.

His sister screamed, and Milo turned his head. Now that he was closer, he could tell it was Harper. She'd been sixteen when he'd left. That made her twenty-six now, but obviously still in need of her big brother's protection.

"Idiot" was right.

Harper looked up at him with lowered brows, and Milo held his breath as he waited for her to recognize him. It didn't take long.

"Milo?"

He opened his arms wide for the hug he knew was coming. It had taken him years, but he was here now, ready to keep her safe.

Some punk thinks he can just kiss my sister. Not on my *watch.*

But Harper didn't move—not toward Milo anyway. She turned her back on him and fussed over the jerk who'd had his mouth all over hers; the same guy who had just been arguing with Audrey minutes earlier, and who had said some rude stuff to Harper. There were a few hushed words exchanged between the two before Harper spun back around to face Milo.

"What is wrong with you?" Harper's furious glare burned him to his core.

Wrong with *him*? He'd only been trying to get this creep away from his sister. They were out in the middle of nowhere, not visible from the inn. The guy had been talking about...well it didn't matter what they'd been talking about, it was dangerous out here. Who knows what could have happened if Milo hadn't stopped things.

The man standing beside Harper wiped his nose. His hand came away free of blood, and Milo's fingers itched to punch him again to make sure he wasn't so lucky the second time. "Who is this bloke?"

He hadn't thought it possible, but his sister's eyes burned even hotter. "It doesn't matter. You're not a part of my life anymore. You can't just march in here and punch the guy I love."

Guy she *loved*?

Even under normal circumstances, this would be an awkward conversation. But jet-lagged and exhausted, it was almost impossible for Milo to make sense of it. Audrey had been thrilled to see him when she'd picked him up at the airport. Seeing Harper's less than enthusiastic greeting was making him doubt this whole crazy idea.

To be fair, Milo hadn't punched anyone Audrey loved.

Yet.

He took a step toward his sister. "Look, I know you're probably mad—"

"Mad doesn't even begin to describe what I'm feeling right now." With her hands balled into fists at her side, she looked scarily like their mother. Who, incidentally, had also been thrilled to see him.

"I thought Sienna was the dramatic one."

"How would you know?"

This was just getting worse and worse. "Look, I didn't come here to fight."

"Could've fooled me," said Harper's guy.

"Nobody asked you." Milo glared at him, but he glared right back.

"I'd rather listen to him than you," Harper spat, and put her hand on Snarky McSnark's arm.

Milo took a deep breath. This was the opposite of what he'd been imagining. "I shouldn't even be out here. The producer told me to stay hidden."

"Bruce knows about this?" Harper looked shocked

for a second, then she shook her head. "Of course. Nothing good comes from that man."

He'd expected his sisters to be shocked, maybe even mad, but this was outright hostile.

"Hey," said the frustratingly non-bloody guy standing next to her. "Bruce is the reason I'm here."

Harper looked up at him with a gooey-eyed expression that Milo could tell was real. He'd seen enough fake ones to know the difference.

Milo cleared his throat. "Care to tell me who you are?"

Harper's doe eyes turned deadly in a heartbeat.

"I'm Austin." The guy didn't stick out his hand. Instead, he tilted his chin up like a challenge. A challenge he'd just lost, judging by the purple bruise starting to blossom across his cheek.

Milo tried not to roll his eyes.

"You don't have to talk to him." Harper folded her arms across her chest.

She might not be a teenager anymore, but boy was she moody. Milo realized he really shouldn't have let anyone see him. "You shouldn't be talking to me, anyway. I'll just go back into the trees, and we'll just pretend you never saw me. Be sure to act surprised later."

He turned to head back to his hiding place, but Harper reached out and grabbed his arm. "You punched my boyfriend and want to pretend like everything is fine? It doesn't work like that."

Milo really didn't think he could take much more. He shook off her hand and pinched the bridge of his nose. The massive headache coming on was not helping his patience.

"I'm telling Bruce about what happened," Harper said.

"Don't!"

Milo was thinking it, but he wasn't the one who said it.

Austin grabbed Harper's arm to stop her from running off. "You know how Bruce is. He's already pissed because I quit. Don't test him tonight. He could send the whole thing up in flames."

Milo held his breath. Of all his sisters, he and Harper had been the most at odds. Maybe because she was the middle girl, or maybe because they were both Capricorns. Almost six years younger, she had been young enough to embarrass him when he brought home dates, but not so young he could brush it off as a silly kid like he could with Sienna.

Harper twisted her mouth into a frown and considered her older brother for a heart-stopping few moments. "Fine, I won't say anything to Bruce."

"Thank you." Milo let out a relieved sigh.

"I'm not doing this for you. I'm doing it for the one decent guy in my life." She reached out to grab Austin's hand and started pulling him back toward the inn. As they walked away, she called out over her shoulder, "But if I were you, I'd stop skulking around in the dark. I'd hate for you to accidentally step on a copperhead."

Milo had to laugh at that. Where he'd been the past ten years, snakes had been the least of his problems.

TWO

4 Days Until Dream Wedding

REAGAN BALLED her hands into fists to keep from slapping someone.

She wanted to scream. But she had never so much as raised her voice or stamped her foot without her mother's voice echoing in her head about the proper conduct of a lady and a champion.

Miss Texas does not yell. She calmly restates her opinion in a more pleasing manner.

Well, Miss Texas had had it up to here with her gorgeous but grouchy fiancé, and he could use a good kick in the rear right about now.

All Reagan wanted was to help Audrey on her big day. They'd promised to be each other's maid of honor their freshman year. That was a solemn oath that had to be respected. Even if your best friend decided to get married in a helicopter or in Siberia or—as Audrey had chosen—on a reality show.

They had four days left in filming and everything that could go wrong, had. People had gone missing, the chef was refusing to cook them anything, and now they were being pulled into a late-night filming session for who knew what reason. It had been the most stressful week of Reagan's life, and she'd been a beauty queen for Pete's sake. At least Audrey had shown up again after causing twenty-four hours of panic. Everyone had been running around like crazy except the producer, who had known the whole time where she'd been and had conveniently forgotten to tell anyone in order to get footage of the bridesmaids' efforts to cover up her absence.

Harry thought it was the final proof that they should leave.

"This is humiliating." His open palm hit the desk in her hotel room. "How do we even know this whole thing will end in a wedding? We could be giving him hours of footage for his new show *The Most Gullible People Alive*."

Reagan bit her tongue. That totally sounded like a show she would binge-watch. She secretly loved reality shows. Being on one herself, however, had proved a little too much to handle, even for her pageant-honed nerves of steel.

"There are only three days left," she said, for the second time in as many minutes. She knew from years of experience that he didn't actually need her to say anything. He would vent, and she would listen quietly, and then it would be over. It was just what she had to put up with to be with someone like Harry. Her mother's voice was there to remind her that *"sacrifices must be made for the life you want. Rich, successful men aren't easy to live with, but it's impossible to live without them."*

Reagan had no intention of living without Harry. Not only would he provide the security Reagan's mom had always wanted for her daughter, but Reagan actually loved him. Unlike her mom and stepdad, she and Harry would be happy together. At least they would be once this whole reality show was over, and they started planning their own wedding.

"Three more days of wasted time."

"It'll be all the fun stuff, I promise." Reagan smiled despite the late hour and the grumpy man in front of her. "There's the dress fittings and picking the flowers and choosing the menu."

"You mean all the stuff the girls get to pick because you won those stupid contests?"

Reagan flushed. The first part of filming had been competitions between the bridesmaids and the groomsmen—and the girls had won a lot. Probably because the groom Eli was so gaga for Audrey that he wanted to be sure she got whatever she wanted for her wedding day. That had also annoyed Harry, who liked to win.

"There's the bachelor and bachelorette parties."

Harry's frown lifted a fraction of an inch. "I could use a party after the week we've had. Hopefully the other guys know where we can get a decent bottle of scotch to celebrate properly."

Reagan kept the smile on her face as she let out a soft sigh. It wasn't that Harry was selfish, not compared to some people, but ever since they arrived at the Emerald Inn, he'd struggled to see past himself. It was understandable, really. He was about to make partner at his father's law firm, and being away from the office at such a critical time in his career could put everything at risk. Their entire future was at stake, but he'd been willing to be here with her. She could handle his extra-grouchiness.

She stood up from her spot on the bed and walked over to Harry. Standing behind him, she wrapped her arms around his chest. "If Eli doesn't know where to get decent scotch, I bet you could teach him."

She'd meant the words to build him up, but Harry pulled away and whipped around. "And that's another thing. When I make partner, we're going to have to talk about who you keep company with."

Reagan's head jerked back. "What?"

"Mrs. Harry Woodly-Huntington does not hang out with schoolteachers and fishermen."

"Fox works on boats, he doesn't actually—"

He waved a hand, and she snapped her mouth shut. "I know you all go way back. College was fun, but it's been over for six years. It's time to move up in the world. When we're married, you can't keep coming up here every other weekend. There'll be events in town, and I'll need my beautiful bride at my side."

Reagan took a deep breath. This was what her mother had wanted for her. An easy life, and the struggles of her childhood left far behind. She loved Harry and wanted to be with him more than anything. If seeing her best friend a little less was what it took, then that was what needed to happen.

But she couldn't let down Audrey, not when it was so close to the end.

Reagan swallowed down her disappointment and fixed her winning pageant smile on her face. "I can't wait to be at your side forever."

His shoulders relaxed, and relief washed across his face.

She stepped toward him, caressed her hand up his arm to wrap it around his bicep, and leaned her head on his shoulder. "What's three more little days in the grand scheme of things?"

She could feel him tense under her. "I hope you appreciate all the sacrifices I'm making for you."

"Absolutely. Thank you so much for being here for our friends."

"Your friends."

Again she bit back her first reply. *Don't contradict your husband*, her mother always warned. Harry had known Eli, Audrey, Wade, and Fox as long as he'd known Reagan—since sophomore year of college—but he'd never seemed to click with them. Sometimes she thought it would have been better if he'd met her freshman year, when Audrey's brother Milo had still been around. He had been that central point around which much of their lives that year had focused. Audrey and Eli were so into each other, Reagan would have been left behind if not for the constant circle of friends whirling around Milo, pulling her along for the ride. If Harry had known everyone from the beginning, maybe he wouldn't be so jealous, and he'd feel like they were his friends too.

If ten days in a remote mountain inn hadn't helped things, maybe nothing would.

"Thank you for helping my friends," she said, and tugged on his hand. "We need to get downstairs. Bruce said they need to shoot a final scene, and the sooner we get it done, the sooner today can be over."

He stepped away from her. "I just need to grab something from my room. See you down there in a few minutes?"

She nodded, and he bent to kiss her cheek. When his

lips touched her skin, she closed her eyes, relishing the brief contact. Other than an occasional peck, Harry hadn't really kissed her in longer than she could remember.

He loves you, she reminded herself, though it sounded more like another lecture from her mother. *He proposed, he wants to spend his life with you. So what if his kisses aren't as passionate as when he was twenty?*

When he pulled away, he frowned. "Be sure to clean yourself up a bit before you go down. You look terrible."

With a weary sigh, she watched him walk out the door. It felt like she spent her whole life waiting for him. The past few years had been an exercise in patience as she spent countless lonely nights while he had been in law school, taken the bar—twice—and then the grueling hours of a junior associate. *It would all be worth it,* both he and her mother had told her countless times. They were picking a day for their own wedding once this whole *Wedding Games* thing was over.

Just a little longer, and I won't have to worry about anything anymore.

She took a quick peek in the mirror and made a face. Harry was right, she did look terrible. Between Sienna's stage experience, Reagan's pageant skills, and the occasional helping hand from the crew of the show, the bridesmaids usually looked great. Unfortunately, there was only so much that makeup could do to cover the exhaustion the past few days had brought on. Her normally bouncy red curls hung limp at her shoulders, and instead of the sparkling porcelain skin that had won her two state titles, her complexion was tinged with gray.

She did her best with what she had on hand and hoped she could stand behind someone. Her mother would be furious if she saw her on TV looking anything other than her normal, perfect self. Not to mention Harry would probably just send her back upstairs if she didn't look the part of a Woodly-Huntington fiancée. The producer would undoubtedly love it. He had mostly left Reagan alone this week, focusing on the bride and the antics of the groomsmen and Sienna. But something told her that an exhausted maid of honor would play right into whatever story he was crafting.

With a final look in the mirror, she headed out. Thoughts of her mother, Harry, and when she could get some much needed beauty sleep swirled around in her head so fast, she almost missed Harper and Austin storming past her down the hall. A purple bruise covered half of Austin's face.

Reagan opened her mouth to ask what was going on, but they brushed by her with barely a glance, too absorbed in their conversation to notice her. She stepped back against the wall to let them by, and her heart sank at the sight of Harper's worried face. Had something happened with Bruce?

Reagan hurried down the stairs into the reception area, her heart pounding. Small groups of crewmembers were milling about, taking things into the conference room where they'd been filming the big scenes. Audrey and Eli were in a corner, and her best friend looked radiant, despite the late hour. Hopefully all the cameras would be on her tonight.

"Excuse me." A voice behind Reagan reminded her that she was blocking the staircase.

"Sorry." She stepped to the side and glanced at the hulk of a man who must be one of the cameramen. Then she whipped her head back and gasped as his massive form retreated up the stairs. The air constricted around her and a swirling, sinking feeling filled her stomach. She hadn't seen that profile in ten years. No wonder Audrey looked so happy.

Milo was back.

THREE

4 Days Until Dream Wedding

"ALRIGHT, alright, let's get things started."

Jason Castle had on more makeup than Milo had ever seen on a human being—and he'd spent four years of college surrounded by sorority girls. Well, almost four years. Thanks to Kylie, he hadn't exactly finished his degree. He took a calming breath. He thought he'd finally let go of all that anger, but just thinking about how one stupid spontaneous decision had altered the last ten years was enough to raise his blood pressure, and he didn't want to get mad now. Not when he was so close to finally having his family back.

"Milo, you wait here until you hear me call your name, okay?" Jason was smiling, his teeth so white they were practically glowing. He was also drawing out his words and looking at Milo with a slightly pitying expression.

"I heard you," he said with a frown.

"I just need to make sure after you left your spot in the woods. Bruce is worried you're a liability."

"And I'm sure Bruce would hate for there to be any

more drama," he said mostly to himself, though he knew Jason had heard when he chuckled in response.

It wasn't a joke, and the false timber of Jason's laugh was like a bullet to Milo's heart. If only he'd been able to recognize fake things like that sooner, he would've been back with his family years ago.

Jason's laugh vanished, and he gave Milo a serious stare. "No one has seen you, right?"

Milo just pressed his lips together, rather than lie. He'd tried to sneak into the inn unseen to chase after Harper and her—ugh—boyfriend. In the flurry of activity, he thought he'd gone unnoticed. But someone from the production crew had been standing at the top of the stairs and rushed him into an empty hotel room to hide him again.

At Milo's silent admission of guilt, Jason's right eyebrow cocked, but without a single wrinkle appearing on his forehead. "Well, this should be fun."

He disappeared through the doors to the dining room and left Milo standing there with the crewmember who hadn't let him out of her sight since he'd snuck into the inn. She was young and wore a lanyard with a badge that read "Jennifer." He ignored her curious stares and instead focused on deciphering what Jason was saying on the other side of the doors. Whatever the words were, he sounded excited, and it was all supremely over-dramatic. Milo was tempted to barge through the doors to skip it all and get to the good part.

But he couldn't do that. He'd already messed up once, and he needed to honor his side of the bargain so he could get the one thing he wanted more than anything else—to be free from Kylie forever and back with his family again.

He was afraid to know what would happen if Bruce found out about his run-in with Harper in the woods. Would he send him back to Australia, without the promised check that would solve all of Milo's problems?

"Okay," Jennifer whispered from beside him as she looked down at her phone. "Bruce is ready to have you walk in any minute now. On my signal, you'll go in."

Milo nodded.

"Now, there will be cameras set up all around the room. One straight in front of you when you walk in, and one on either side of you. It's important that you don't look at them."

"Uh-huh." Milo doubted he'd even notice the cameras. He'd be too busy looking for Sienna. She was the only sister he hadn't seen yet, and he was anxious to know if her reaction would be more like Harper or Audrey. His fingers tapped against his thigh.

Jennifer huffed loudly. "Are you even listening?"

He wanted to say that he'd heard every word, but he was so consumed by his thoughts, it was possible he missed something. "Did I miss my cue?"

The woman rolled her eyes. "Bruce said he was worried you were going to be as difficult as your sisters, but—"

Her voice stopped as Milo took a couple of slow steps toward her. "Excuse me?"

Jennifer took a step back and quickly looked down at her phone. "Oh, look at that. It's time to go in." She paused for a second before adding, "For the love of everything, please don't look at the cameras."

Milo took another calming breath. But this time, he was trying to slow his heart to keep it from bursting from his chest. He opened the door and tried to smile, but it faltered when he walked into the room and felt the eyes of a dozen different people on him.

Audrey was grinning from ear to ear. Eli and Fox were standing with their arms crossed, peering at him suspiciously, while Wade bounced on his feet with happiness. Harper glowered like Milo knew she would, and Sienna shrieked so loudly, Milo was sure an eardrum has burst.

The bone crushing hug from his youngest sister was a surprise.

"Oof, you've gotten strong." He had to take a step back or risk toppling over from her enthusiasm.

"Well when you left, I was only twelve." He could barely hear her with her face pressed into his chest in the tightest hug he'd had in years.

"I know. I'm sorry."

"I'm sure you had a good reason." She took a step back and beamed up at him with tears in her eyes. "You're here now, that's what counts. And you'll get to see Audrey get married!"

While the cameras circled them, she launched into a detailed description of everything they'd done so far on the show to get ready for Audrey's big day. Milo tried to focus on her words, but he'd already heard most of it from Audrey in the car on the way to the inn. She'd caught him up on everything in her life, while Milo had stayed vague on the details of his. All she needed to know was that he'd gone to Australia thinking he was doing the right thing and had been too embarrassed to call when things had gone south. Which was the truth, and luckily she hadn't pushed too hard for more. She'd been happy to keep talking about her and Eli, and the wedding.

Her excited babbling had been nearly identical to Sienna's, Milo realized with a smile. Sienna took his expression as encouragement and kept going in her story. It was like she was twelve again and wanted to tell him about her day at school. The shock of seeing her all grown up would take a few days to wear off.

"Sienna, I think that's enough." Fox was suddenly at her side, his hand on her shoulder. "The rest of us want to say hi, too."

Milo's eyes zeroed in on that hand and swallowed down his sudden protective rage. Audrey had mentioned that there was something going on between Fox and Sienna, but she was still twelve in his mind, and Fox was his old friend—emphasis on the old. When Fox, Eli, and Wade had joined the rugby team as freshmen in college, Milo was the captain who took them through initiation.

Now that freshman had his hands all over Milo's youngest sister.

"Fox," said Milo gruffly, holding out a hand. Fox shook it, then looped an arm around his shoulder to slap him twice on the back, a little harder than was strictly necessary.

Milo squeezed his hand tightly in response. "So you've met my baby sister Sienna?"

Fox paled slightly but kept his chin up and nodded. After another beat and careful look, Milo released his hand.

Someone from the crew ushered the happy couple off to one side, then guided Milo toward the rest of his friends and family. They were all arranged in a semi-circle around the room.

"It's like a receiving line at a wedding," Audrey said

when he stopped in front of her. "You get to greet all your guests."

Not that I'd had one at mine, he thought bitterly. *Or any guests of my own.*

If there was a pill to wipe all bad memories from his brain, he'd take it in a heartbeat.

"I'm the guest." With effort, he managed to get a smile back on his face. "I can't wait to see my beautiful sister walk down the aisle."

Then Milo turned to Eli. "Took you guys long enough." He slapped Eli on the back, much gentler than Fox had done with him.

When Milo figured out a way to ditch the cameras, he wanted to take a moment to tell Eli what it meant to know that he'd been there for his sister. Milo would never have been able to leave unless he thought his sisters would be okay without him, and Eli was a big reason for that.

Milo held out a hand to Wade, who was standing next to Eli. "This larrikin is still around?"

Wade's eyebrows drew together. "I'll take that as a compliment, I guess." He grinned. "They can't get rid of me, no matter what they do. I'm like that piece of chewing gum stuck to your shoe."

"Tell me about it." Milo laughed and shook his head. Wade had been like that on the rugby team, a piece of gum sticking to their opponents or the ball as needed. "Are you still playing?"

"Nope, just a boring programmer now, like my dad."

"Hardly boring. That takes a lot of hard work." Milo tried not to let the jealousy shine through in his voice. Audrey and Eli had both gotten their master's in teaching, Milo knew from his mom that Harper was running her own business, and Sienna was pursuing her acting dreams in New York. Wade was doing great as well. Everyone had achieved so much.

Meanwhile, Milo would be starting over again at the ripe old age of thirty-two. An age when he should be settled in a career. So, while leaving before his final semester had ended had been the biggest mistake of Milo's life for a whole host of reasons, the loss of a career he loved was the worst.

Next up was Harper, whose arms were folded so tightly against her chest, he worried she would hurt herself. With a camera hovering over his shoulder, Milo raised his eyebrows in a silent plea.

"I'm sorry," he said, hoping she would know it was for the punch to her boyfriend's face, not just the ten-year absence. He held out his arms and hoped she could do this for Audrey. This show, as ridiculous as it was turning out to be, was what she wanted. Milo hoped that Harper could put aside whatever competitive streak kept the two of them at odds and give in, just for once.

This time, she did open her arms to him. But the hug she gave him was so brief, Milo could practically hear the voiceover. *Some family members were less quick to forgive than others*. He'd have to get her on her own at some point to explain it all. It was so frustrating not being able to say what he really wanted to because of the cameras. The producer wanted drama, but Milo wasn't about to lay out his whole life story for national TV to laugh at his idiocy. He'd let Harper enjoy hearing about the long list of his failures in private.

Milo turned away from his sister, and his gaze fell on the gorgeous redhead he'd passed earlier in the hall. He'd been so focused on Harper that he hadn't realized right away who she was. But seeing her now, with her bright smile and deep blue eyes, it hit him all at once.

"Reagan?"

The tinkle of her laugh sent a shockwave through his body.

"Do I really look that different?" Her cheeks flushed a deep pink. Like the ocean being pulled into high tide by the moon, he leaned toward her, unable to stay away. She let out a surprised "oh" when he gathered her into his arms.

"You look amazing," he said. He pulled out of the hug and took an even better look at her. She seemed tired, but so did everyone. Unlike everyone else, however, she practically radiated from within. He remembered she'd been a beauty queen back in the day, but it was more than good posture and shining hair. She'd been beautiful inside and out, even as a sassy, smart-mouthed freshman.

"Yikes, how awful did I look in college then?" The twinkle in her eyes caught him off guard. He had forgotten how sharp she could be.

"You always looked amazing, Miss America." The corner of his mouth lifted when she rolled her eyes at the nickname.

"No one's called me that since college, Cousin It."

He chuckled and ran a hand through his longer-than-usual locks. "I didn't exactly have time for a trip to the salon."

She leaned in and inhaled deeply. "You could have at least showered."

Laughter rumbled deeper in his chest. For the first time since he'd arrived, he felt something close to the happiness he'd been hoping to find. Before he could examine why it was from exchanging a few words with Reagan and not from seeing his family again, someone nearby cleared his throat.

"Excuse me."

Milo turned his attention to a guy not much taller than Reagan, with dark hair parted to one side. From his expensively casual t-shirt and jeans to the way he looked down (or rather up, given their height difference) his nose at Milo, his entire demeanor screamed lawyer. The last time he'd seen a lawyer was when he was sitting across the table from Kylie.

Milo did not like lawyers.

The cameraman coughed behind him, and Milo bit back his first response. "I don't think we've met." He held out a hand.

The guy ignored it and instead put his arm around Reagan. She leaned into him automatically, like it was a pose for a camera. It probably was, given the situation they were in. But the glimmer from her eyes was gone, and she seemed to fade into the background when he opened his mouth.

"I'm Harry Woodly-Huntington." He said it like Milo should recognize the name.

Milo balled his hand into a fist but let it drop to his side. He'd already punched one person today. Two seemed a little excessive, even for a reality wedding show.

Harry pursed his lips when his name didn't get the reaction he'd expected. "I'm Reagan's fiancé."

All the air left Milo's chest in a heartbeat. His glance flickered down to Reagan's hand and the gigantic diamond that sparkled there. It was the kind of ostentatious ring a total tool would get for his bride-to-be. He shook his head. First Harper, now Reagan. Sienna was the only one of his sisters who had managed to find a decent guy.

Reagan's not *your sister,* he reminded himself. But she was his sister's best friend, which made it normal to have this protective urge for her, right?

Judging by the possessive grasp Harry had on Reagan, and the way she evaporated under his touch, no one had protected her properly in a long time.

4 Days Until Dream Wedding

THE SECOND THAT Bruce said they were done for the evening, Harry led Reagan upstairs. With his tight grip on her elbow, she could barely wave goodnight to the other girls. She carefully avoided looking at Milo, knowing Harry's mood probably had something to do with Audrey's brother and his sudden appearance.

"What was *that*?" Harry snapped once they were in her hotel room and safely out of earshot of any cameras.

"What?" Reagan sat on the edge of her bed, her legs crossed at the ankles. For the second time that night, Reagan knew she'd have to calm Harry down. All she wanted to do was sleep, but things had to be smoothed over or it would just get worse. Harry could hold onto grudges like no one else.

"How dare you flirt with someone in front of me. In front of *cameras*." Two spots of red appeared on his cheeks. He paced the small room, hands balled into fists.

Reagan wanted to laugh at the ridiculousness of

Harry's statement, but he'd always felt possessive of her. Even so much as an extra long look at a waiter could set Harry off. She just needed to explain who Milo was since Harry hadn't met him before he disappeared all those years ago.

"I was saying hi to an old friend. It's Audrey's brother, for goodness sake, he was like my brother freshman year."

"He wasn't looking at you like you were his sister."

Reagan took a deep breath.

It wasn't that Harry was a jerk. He'd been picked on as a kid, so he was always working hard to prove himself. With two older brothers, he'd been the little brother they snubbed and who could never live up to them. It was taking him twice as long as it had them to make partner. Having Reagan on his arm when his brothers were both unmarried made him so proud—something he'd told her a hundred times.

"He knows I'm yours." Her hand went automatically to fidget with the ring on her left hand. She'd been hoping for something simple and vintage, like Audrey's ruby ring that had belonged to Eli's grandmother. Reagan's heavy, showy band of diamonds had one goal: let the world know she was taken. She had been so proud to show her mother. And Harry had picked it, so of course she loved it. She loved him.

Which was why she couldn't let it show she was still thinking about Milo's hug. She pushed down the warmth that spread from her chest at the memory of his arms around her and smiled up at Harry. "I know how lucky I am to be yours."

"You've got that right." He finally stopped pacing to

kneel in front of her, and he took her hands in his and kissed them. "I just go crazy when I see guys staring at you like that."

Reagan's chest swelled at the way he looked at her. He did care about her, even if he had an intense way of showing it sometimes. She put a hand on his cheek and rolled her eyes. "He wasn't staring. The cameras were on us, where else was he supposed to look? My feet?"

Harry glanced down and frowned. "Those heels are a little too high, don't you think?"

She slipped them off and pushed them under the bed. "I'm sorry, I was so tired earlier. I'll wear flats tomorrow." She mentally crossed her fingers that would be enough.

He grunted his approval and stood up. "Well, you've kept me up late enough with all this nonsense. I have to be up early for a call. Can you bring me some breakfast tomorrow if I don't come down?"

She nodded, and he left without another word. When the door clicked closed behind him, she let out her breath in a whoosh and flopped onto the bed.

Had she been flirting?

She hadn't talked like that to another guy in what felt like ages. Since she met Harry, she'd been careful to not give anyone the impression she was interested. Harry was too precious to her to risk over something silly like girls drink free nights at the local club, or tutoring guys in business classes. Most of her interactions were with Audrey and Harper. Even her job as a freelance marketing consultant meant she worked at home and did most of her work online. She focused on small businesses that were women-owned because that was where her referrals had led her, and that's what

Harry preferred. All that kept her from having any one-on-one business meetings with men. She wouldn't even know how to flirt if she wanted to since she was so out of practice.

Besides, that was how she'd always talked to Milo. Not that they'd talked extensively or anything when they'd all hung out in a group during college. He'd invite Audrey to his games and the parties with his rugby friends, then stop by to make sure she and Eli were behaving themselves. Milo's teasing had kept Reagan from feeling too much like the third wheel, but had always firmly been in the sisterly range of pestering.

Okay, so maybe she'd had a *tiny* crush on him back then, but it had disappeared almost as soon as he'd left. And just because his hug had made her feel like coming home after a long time away didn't mean that crush was back. She was just nostalgic for freshman year, like anyone would be ten years later and about to watch her best friend get married—and about to get married herself.

Still, it would be a good idea to keep her interactions with him to a minimum over these final days of filming. There'd be so much else going on, Reagan didn't want to have to manage Harry too. Milo probably wouldn't be doing much with the bridesmaids anyway, would he?

———

"LAST NIGHT WAS REALLY GREAT, MILO." Bruce looked across the table and flashed his teeth at Milo. It was almost a smile, in the way that a snake was almost a rabbit.

"Yeah?" Milo raised an eyebrow that felt like it

weighed a ton. It was earlier than he normally got up, and he'd gotten to bed past midnight, plus his body still didn't quite know what time it was. The mug of coffee he'd managed to sweet talk the chef into giving him was the only thing keeping him from floating off into space.

"I mean, the looks Harper was giving you were priceless. Did she always hate you so much?" Bruce seemed giddy at the idea.

Milo took a sip of coffee and stared at the producer. Why did Milo always seem to attract people who reveled in others' pain? He shook his head. "No."

Bruce looked down at a stack of papers. "I've cleared the schedule this morning to get some one-on-one time with you and each of the bridesmaids."

"Just my sisters or all of them?" Milo couldn't help but ask.

Bruce's lips turned up in a half smile. "Would all of them be okay with you?"

Milo nodded but said nothing. The hitch in his chest at the thought of seeing Reagan without her tool of a fiancé around had to be from too much caffeine. Was it stronger in the states? He couldn't remember.

"You are by far the easiest Hudson to work with." He leaned over and slapped Milo on the shoulder. "If you could get that youngest sister of yours to fall in line, that would make my job a lot easier."

The undercurrent of a threat made Milo's stomach clench. Audrey had told him of all the pressure they'd been under, trying to make sure that Bruce got what he wanted for the show. There were clauses built into the contract that would keep her from getting the wedding she'd been dreaming of, and Milo would do everything in his power to make sure it happened. That was the reason for flying halfway across the world. The promise of enough money to finally pay off his debts and free him from the life he'd been trapped in for ten years had been too tempting to ignore, no matter the strings attached.

Family came first. He'd ignored that once, and it had turned out worse than he could have ever imagined.

"If you want me to talk some sense into Sienna, it'll need to be off camera." Milo had made his brief apologies the previous night, but under the harsh lights and gaze of the cameras, he hadn't said all he wanted to. They needed to know more about why he left, and Bruce needed juicy footage, but there had to be a way that didn't end with Milo baring all his past shame to the world.

Bruce's eyes narrowed. "That's not what we agreed. You promised everything on camera, and I promised a check."

"I haven't seen my sisters in a decade. That doesn't deserve ten minutes alone to apologize privately?"

Bruce leaned back in his chair and crossed his arms over his chest. "You had the entire car ride with Audrey. That was more than generous considering the terms of our contract."

"And you're smart enough to see that my other two sisters would need an entire cross-country trip to sort out what we've got going on. Ten minutes off camera with them will still leave you plenty of the good stuff."

Milo held his breath as the older man considered this. In his flashy suit and oily hair, he looked as out of place in the mountains of North Carolina as Milo felt.

His head knew he was home, but his body craved more time outside. The taste he'd gotten of the fresh mountain air the previous night hadn't been nearly enough. Maybe he could negotiate these private talks outside.

Though Harper would probably just run away from him.

"You can have ten minutes in the safe room," Bruce said after a lengthy pause.

Milo sat up straight, pleased he'd gotten what he'd wanted so easily.

"Thank you," he said, and he meant it. "I'm sorry to take almost an hour from your filming schedule."

Bruce shook his head. "Not ten minutes each. Ten minutes total, all of them together."

Milo swallowed a groan. Of course there'd be a catch. He'd have to figure out a way to focus the conversation, so Sienna didn't take over, and Harper wouldn't waste time yelling at him. She could do that on camera. Bruce would love it, but Milo needed her to listen.

"All three?" Milo didn't want any other misunderstandings.

"All four." Bruce flashed his teeth again and something shifted in Milo's chest.

If he'd had a protective urge seeing Harry lord over Reagan, the thought of Bruce involving her in his schemes set Milo on fire.

Both men stood up from the table, and Milo stuck out his hand. Bruce shook it, then left. Jennifer the loyal production assistant trailed behind him taking notes as he spat out new plans for the day.

Milo had his own plans to make. He'd have only ten minutes to both make his case with Harper and figure out how he could protect Reagan from whatever was happening in her life that had made her go from the bubbly and bright girl he remembered to this scared and shy woman these brutes thought they could control.

FIVE

3 Days Until Dream Wedding

MARCEY MUST NOT BE mad anymore, Reagan thought as she picked at the fresh fruit on her plate. The Emerald Inn's chef had been understandably upset when Sienna and Fox's "argument" a few days ago had ended with smashed plates all over the floor. The disagreement had all been a show for the cameras, but the chef's irritation had been real. Reagan's own irritation flared when she looked down at the text that Harry had sent earlier that morning.

Busy on a call all morning. Don't disturb me by bringing me breakfast. I'll get something later.

It wasn't like Reagan was going to try to talk to him or anything. She knew better than that. Would bringing a plate of eggs and bacon really "disturb" his call that much?

It must be the cameras. If she had someone trailing behind her with a walkie-talkie, that could make a bad impression on whoever Harry was talking to. It was probably a client or his dad. As much as she needed to see him right now, Reagan didn't want to risk it.

She's almost convinced herself that her feelings weren't hurt when the next text came through.

Make sure you don't forget to wear flats.

She sighed as she looked down at the shoes she'd worn for the day. While they weren't the three-inch heel stilettos from the night before, she worried that the tiny half-inch kitten heel might be enough to push an already on-edge Harry over the cliff.

Reagan took one more bite of honeydew before grabbing her things. She had just enough time to run upstairs to her room and change into something with less height-enhancing qualities before the start of the day's activities.

She was walking out the door when she heard Audrey's voice calling out.

"Reagan, come quick."

The urgency in her tone stopped Reagan in her tracks and sent her heart racing. This stupid show made it impossible to ever relax fully. There was always something, and Reagan wasn't sure if this was another plot twist dreamed up by the King of Pain himself, Bruce Bigg, or a real emergency.

"What's up?"

"It's Milo."

Reagan's heart leaped at his name. "Is he okay?"

Audrey started moving her arms back and forth like she was trying to pull Reagan by a rope. "Yes, but he only has ten minutes of guaranteed no-camera time in the safe room and has asked for all of the bridesmaids to be there."

"Even me?"

"Yes, you're like a sister to us, and he's hoping to quickly explain why he's been gone for so long without the cameras."

Like a sister. Yes, that's what Reagan was to Milo, and that was for the best.

"But we have to go now." Audrey tugged on Reagan's hand. "His ten minutes are about to start."

Reagan nodded. "Yeah. Okay."

She started trailing behind Audrey, their hands still entwined, when she heard her name again.

"Reagan, where are you going?" Harry was standing at the other end of the hall with his hands on his hips and a glare on his face. "I finished my call early just to eat breakfast with you."

She stopped in her tracks, which made Audrey stumble.

"We're going to talk to Milo," the bride-to-be answered. "We get ten minutes with him in the safe room. And it's already started."

The vein in Harry's forehead started throbbing, and Reagan could have smacked Audrey for mentioning her brother's name in front of Harry after what happened— or rather, what Harry imagined happened—the night before. "You're sneaking off to a secret room with Milo?"

"And Audrey and Harper and Sienna," Reagan added quickly.

"I don't care who else is there." He lifted his hands. "Think about how that will look for the cameras."

"The cameras aren't there right now." Audrey looked down at her phone and tugged on Reagan's hand. "But they will be in eight minutes. Come on."

Reagan's head turned back and forth between

Audrey and Harry. Audrey's eyes were pleading as she bounced on her feet, eager for Reagan to follow her. Harry's face was red while his stare penetrated deep down into Reagan's soul.

"I, uh…" She bit her bottom lip. "I'll try to make it, but I need to talk to Harry really fast first."

Audrey released Reagan's hand and let out a long sigh. "Make it really, *really* fast. I doubt Bruce is going to give us another opportunity like this. And I promise you're going to want to hear what he has to say."

Of course Reagan wanted to hear what Milo had to say. He up and left ten years ago and no one had heard from him since. What reason could he possibly have for doing that? It must have been good for Audrey to forgive him so easily.

But Reagan wasn't one of the Hudson sisters, and she had other responsibilities she needed to tend to first, like her fiancé. She watched Audrey race down the hall toward the safe room, before turning to face Harry whose vein and red face had not gone down even a little.

"How was the call?"

He shook his head, his lips in a thin, hard line. "Do you think I want to talk about my call when you were about to do something so stupid?"

"Audrey said there weren't any cameras."

"And you believe her? Honestly, Reagan, how you manage to run a business when you trust everyone instantly is beyond me. I'm constantly having to swoop in and save you from agreeing to bad deals."

"I don't need you to—"

He laughed, though the sound wasn't a joyful one. "If you don't need me, then why am I still here?"

Reagan took a step toward Harry. "You know that's

not what I was going to say. And besides, you have to stay. You're one of the groomsmen."

"Don't you think Milo will be the third groomsman now that's he's back to save the day?"

Harry's voice was bitter, and Reagan hated seeing him like this. He was under so much pressure, and there was so much history between everyone here. He probably felt even more left out now that Milo was here.

She put on her brightest smile. "Even if Milo is the third groomsmen, I still need you. You're my fiancé, and there's no one else I'd rather be with to celebrate my best friend's wedding."

Not even with Milo and his warm, welcoming arms.

Milo was unreliable. He might not even stay long enough to see his sister get married. For all Reagan knew, he'd be gone tomorrow, leaving broken hearts in his wake. He was the complete opposite of Harry. Her fiancé was steady and stable. Her early life had been so uncertain; she needed her future to be grounded in something solid. Plus, Harry loved Reagan in his own way, even if he was difficult sometimes.

Reagan pushed up on her toes and pressed her lips to Harry's cheek. "Don't go. It's only three more days. We're over halfway through *Wedding Games*. When we get back home, we can get a reservation for your favorite restaurant and put all of this craziness behind us."

He grunted in response.

"You'll see," Reagan said, pulling back and putting her hand on his cheek. "You'll see. One day, we'll look back at this and laugh."

Harry leaned into her touch and turned his face toward the ground. His head stayed like that for all of three seconds, before it snapped back up. "I thought you were wearing flats today."

Reagan sighed. "I forgot. I was going back up to my room to change when Audrey caught me."

Harry shook his head and opened his mouth to say something when his phone started buzzing. He looked down at the screen and back at Reagan. "I've got to take this. Go change, and I'll meet you at whatever stupid thing we have to do today."

Harry marched down the hall and out of sight. It would be good for everyone if she forgot all about the secret meeting that was taking place between Milo and the rest of the bridesmaids right now. The best thing for her to do was to run up to her room as she originally planned and change her shoes.

But as she looked up at the clock on the wall and saw that she still had four minutes to get there, Reagan realized she didn't want to do what was best.

For the first time in a long time, she wanted to be reckless, and she was pretty sure Milo was to blame.

————

"AUSTRALIA?" Sienna shrieked and smacked her hands against Milo's chest. "You've been down under for ten years, and you didn't think that your sisters might want to come visit?"

Milo didn't even flinch at Sienna's wimpy effort to hit him. "No, I honestly didn't. Strewth, I figured you all were so mad at me, it was best to stay away."

"You got that right." Harper was in the farthest corner of the small room, her arms folded across her chest. Her glare from the previous night was back with a vengeance.

Audrey made a huffing noise. "She doesn't mean that. Why would you think that?"

He took a deep breath. He didn't want to tell them everything, but he had to tell them something. "Because I was so mad at myself for leaving."

Sienna's eyes went a little watery, and Audrey practically cooed.

"Then why did you?" Harper said, her voice like a slap.

"I thought that I had to. But it was all a lie."

Audrey tilted her head. "This is about Kylie, isn't it?"

Milo had managed to avoid all mention of where he'd been while in the car with Audrey, but of course she'd make the connection once she learned he'd been in Australia.

Harper raised an eyebrow at this. "Who's Kylie?"

"No one," he said quickly, and turned to face the shelves that lined one wall. He lay a hand on one, but it made a creaking noise, and he quickly removed it. The last thing he needed was to have the whole thing collapse on him and have the crash bring the entire crew to the door.

"It was for a girl?" Sienna's voice broke a little. "You loved someone more than us, just like—"

"No!" He turned and wrapped his little sister into his arms. "I loved all of you more than anything. I still do. I thought you didn't need a big brother hanging around anymore."

Sienna sniffed into his chest.

He gave her a squeeze. "I was just a dumb kid. I was like, twenty-two."

She pulled back and smacked his chest again. "Hey! I'm twenty-two."

"And much smarter than I ever was." He smiled and planted a kiss on the top of her head. "Fox seems like the same, good guy I remember from college."

"He's been through his own share of bad choices," Sienna said. "But he made it through, with help from his friends."

Milo felt a weird tug of jealousy. He'd been totally friendless when he'd needed it. He always wondered if he'd just been able to stay in contact with one person if everything would have been different.

He closed his eyes and inhaled deeply. *You're almost free now. It's all in the past.*

"We've got like, four minutes, so was there anything else?" Harper's harsh words reminded him that even with one set of troubles almost in the past, he still had a lot to take care of in the present.

"Yes," he said and opened his eyes. "What's been going on with all of you? You both get two minutes to give me the CliffsNotes version. I already know what's happening with Audrey." He winked at her, and he was relieved to see her smile back. He thought he'd never see that smile again.

Just as Harper opened her mouth, Reagan burst into the room.

"Sorry I'm late! What did I miss?" She closed the door behind her.

"Milo was telling us why he was gone for so long," Sienna answered.

When Reagan turned to face her—undoubtedly seeing Sienna's tear-streaked face—she frowned and stared at Milo with narrowed eyes. "Are you going to break their hearts again, Milo Hudson? Because you can just go right back to wherever you've been hiding if that's the case."

Everyone in the room stared at Reagan with open mouths and wide eyes—including Milo.

She flushed a deep pink and dropped her hand. "What?"

"I haven't heard you talk like that to anyone in years." Audrey's lips twitched. "Especially to a guy."

Sienna snickered. "I like sassy Reagan. Where's she been hiding?"

Reagan shrank back against the door. "Oh, I'm sorry, I didn't mean to be rude."

"Don't worry, Milo just has that talent to bring it out in everyone," Harper said.

Milo fought the urge to stick his tongue out at her. Instead, he focused his attention on Reagan. "It's fine. It's been an emotional few days for everyone. How have you been?"

"Um, fine, thank you."

The spark that he'd seen in her was completely extinguished almost immediately after surfacing. He didn't think he liked this shy and demure version of Reagan, and Audrey made it sound like that was who Reagan was these days. She looked like a shadow of the girl he once knew.

"I was just hearing from the girls everything they've been up to lately." He gave her a smile. "You're getting married too, right? When's the big day?" If she was anything like Audrey, she'd spend hours telling him all the details of the proposal and the planning so far.

Unlike her best friend, however, the question made Reagan shrink back even more. "Oh, you know, Harry is so busy, and focused on work, there hasn't really been time to settle on anything."

"But you must be excited, right?"

"Of course, he's great, really great. Such a gentleman, mother was so proud when I brought him home."

Milo noticed Audrey's frown from the corner of his eye. So he wasn't the only one who got bad vibes from this Harry guy—or was unhappy with how Reagan acted when she talked about him. The pain and fear that he saw in Reagan was so familiar. He'd seen it before—in himself.

The overwhelming urge to protect was back again. Reagan's pale face and trembling hands were like a punch to his gut, and he knew he was in trouble. The thought of anyone making these girls unhappy made him furious.

Milo's hands formed into fists at his side. "Where is—"

Knocking on the door cut his question off, and that was for the best. He was about to ask where Harry was. But why? So Milo could punch him? Deep down, Milo knew the answer to his pent up anger wasn't to go around and start hitting people—well, more people—at his sister's wedding festivities.

But it would feel so bloody good to finally give someone like Harry what he deserved. Kylie never had to pay for her misdeeds, and Milo certainly would never lay a hand on her.

"Ten minutes are up," called a female voice from the other side of the door. It sounded like Jennifer, the production assistant who was attached to Bruce's hip.

Audrey looked down at her phone and frowned. "We still have another minute."

"What are we going to do? Talk about Harry some more? Or maybe listen to Milo give excuses for being a terrible brother?" Harper huffed. "I, for one, am thankful we can end this charade. I need to spend some time with Austin before the next activity."

Austin. Milo already hated that guy. Just not as much as Harry.

Harper flung open the door and marched down the hall, managing to bump Jennifer on her way out, who glared at Harper with more intensity than the situation merited. Milo's urge to defend flared again, but he knew better than to mess with anyone on Bruce's crew. Audrey and Sienna followed Harper out the door.

Milo knew he should go after Harper and try to talk. Things needed to be fixed with Harper, but all it took was a glance at Reagan worrying her bottom lip, and all he could think about was how to protect the beautiful redhead that his sisters considered family. In the short time he'd been reunited with Harper, it was obvious she could take care of herself. Meanwhile, Reagan looked like she was terrified of the world—or at least of being in here alone with Milo.

What had this guy Harry done to make her fear five minutes alone with an old friend?

Jennifer cleared her throat, and Milo dragged himself out into the hallway to find Jason Castle and a cameraman waiting for them.

"Alright, alright," Jason said once the light on the camera started blinking. "The bridal boutique is ready for you to come try on dresses. You can pick one person to go with you."

Instantly, Reagan and Sienna perked up at the mention of going shopping. Milo bit back a grin.

Audrey directed her gaze to Milo. "I want my big brother to come with me."

Both the other girls' shoulders drooped when Audrey spoke, and Milo was ready to argue, but he knew he needed to be the perfect brother when the cameras were rolling. He needed to be the perfect brother after what he did to his sisters—and was still doing to Harper, apparently.

So he forced the corners of his mouth to lift into a smile. "I'd be happy to."

SIX

3 Days Until Dream Wedding

REAGAN BREATHED in the smell of wood and hay and smiled.

Harry's frowning face suddenly filled her field of vision. "What are you doing out here?"

With a concentrated effort honed through many years of walking in sky-high heels in swimsuits, Reagan kept the smile on her face and tried not to let her disappointment at his rough tone shine through.

The groomsmen were supposed to set up the barn for the wedding reception while the cameras filmed, and Reagan had been stealthily following behind them on the trail waiting for the right moment to make her surprise appearance. Judging by the way Harry was staring at her now, however, it wasn't the pleasant surprise for him she was hoping it would be.

"I wanted to see you." She laid a hand on his arm. "I missed you."

He shrugged off her hand, and his eyes trailed down her body and back up in a quick appraisal. "What are you wearing?"

Reagan looked down at her outfit. The running shorts were new, and the t-shirt was from a 5k she and Audrey had run together a few months earlier. It was part of "Operation: Get Fit for the Wedding," and Reagan thought it would be a fun homage to her best friend when the show finally aired. "Workout clothes?"

She hated how it came out as a question.

"You look like a lazy college student or some middle-aged mom who has given up on looking nice anymore. I know you have drawers full of nice Lululemon stuff you can wear."

But I don't want to wear the Lululemon right now. She sighed. "You're right. I can go change."

"Or even better, you could go back to the inn and not be part of this humiliating task." He sighed, and his head dropped back. "Why don't you just spend the afternoon with Sienna or Harper?"

Reagan would have loved more time with either of the Hudson sisters, but Harper was currently busy making up for lost time with Austin while Sienna and her mom were having some one-on-one mother-daughter time.

That left Reagan on her own. Between her remote work and Harry's schedule, she was used to it. But right now, she wanted to be around people—specifically Harry. It was time to try to rekindle some of the passion that had disappeared ever since coming to the Emerald Inn.

Reagan stuck out her lower lip. "They're busy. And besides, I thought it would make it a little more personal if I helped."

Harry shook his head. "Oh, yeah. Because doing the

jobs of the inn's incompetent staff is something that will make a difference to Audrey or Eli."

Reagan put her hand on his arm again. "Harry, please."

He closed his eyes and inhaled deeply. "Fine. Help away."

Reagan nearly squealed out loud at her small victory, but settled for a respectably demure smile of gratitude. While Harry stayed firmly planted in his spot at the edge of the barn, she started grabbing some of the folding chairs. Fox and Wade passed by, carrying a long wooden table to the other side.

"Oh, hey, Reagan," Fox said with a smile. "I didn't realize you were going to be out here with the groomsmen."

Harry snorted loud enough for everyone to hear, and Reagan turned to give him a "please, be good" look. He rolled his eyes, but picked up a single chair and started to walk over to them, slower than molasses in winter. She turned and smiled at Fox and Wade. "Yeah, I thought it might be fun."

"You have some crazy ideas of fun." Wade chuckled. "But I'm glad you're here. Fox and I have no idea what we're doing."

Harry made a snide comment, making sure it was loud enough to hear the sarcastic tone across the barn, but too soft to make out the words. Not that she, Fox, or Wade needed to hear what he said. The message was clear. Harry would be helping as little as possible. Any chance of Reagan reviving any warm and gooey feelings with him were long gone.

It hadn't always been like this. Those first months together had been incredible. He'd gone out of his way to woo her. The whirlwind had lasted through senior year of college, when the hope of a proposal had been dashed by his announcement of going to law school out of state. Reagan's mother would not accept defeat that easily, and got Reagan's stepdad to find her a job in the same town as Harry's school. Reagan had been willing to put in the effort and time then, and it had paid off. Not only for her relationship with Harry, but that was how she got started in the marketing world. What should have been the end turned into a great beginning. She could still make something positive come from this experience too. She just had to try a little harder.

But she didn't want to put up with his grouchiness if she didn't have to.

Reagan smiled at Fox. "Then it's a good thing I'm here."

She looked around the barn. It was perfect for the rustic chic wedding that Audrey and Eli were having, and by the looks of it, the crew of *Wedding Games* even gave them decent materials to work with.

I wonder if there's a catch?

Reagan sighed. Whatever Bruce had in mind, it was too late to change anything now. At least she could make the barn look nice. "If the wedding is going to be on the hillside, looking over the valley, then that means we can use this entire space for the reception."

Fox and Wade nodded their heads, but their eyes were already glazing over.

Reagan laughed at their confused expressions. "Honestly, what were you planning on doing after setting that one table down? Be done for the day?"

They shrugged and gave her sheepish smiles.

Reagan tapped her finger against her lips. "Okay. So you guys won the music challenge."

"Heck yeah, we did." Wade tipped his chin up. "And we've got the footage to prove it."

"Calm down. I'm not disputing that." She rolled her eyes. "The reason I'm asking is, are you guys putting together a playlist meant for dancing, or not?"

The guys looked at each other.

"Uh." Fox scratched his cheek.

"Dancing, obviously." Wade flashed his white teeth in a dazzling smile and waggled his eyebrows.

Reagan felt a smile tugging at her lips. "Good. Then that means we need to keep some space for a dance floor." She looked around the barn and pointed to one corner. "What if we put it over there?"

"Yep. That's what I was thinking too," Wade said.

Fox nudged him with his elbow. "You weren't even thinking about a dance floor."

"Prove it." Wade pushed him back playfully, and soon they were caught up in a fake wrestling match that had Reagan giggling.

Harry would never do something so juvenile, especially not on television, but it was fun watching these old friends act like the same stupid college kids they were back in the day. They were only missing Milo.

Reagan let her mind wander to Audrey and her brother. Did he really come all this way just to go dress shopping with her? Reagan still couldn't believe her best friend had forgiven him so easily. She must have missed something when she showed up late to story time in the safe room. Sienna had been crying, and Harper had been pissed by the time Reagan had finally gotten there.

She'd have to get the full story from Audrey later tonight.

Still goofing off, the guys bumped into Reagan. In a spectacularly graceless fall that her former ballet teacher would be ashamed of, she fell in a lump onto the hard floor of the barn. The guys immediately stopped shoving each other and rushed to help.

"Oops, sorry, Reagan." Wade held out a hand. His face was puckered in an apologetic expression. "That looked like it hurt."

"I'm fine." She really was. Graceless as it had been, she still knew how to fall like a pro. She dusted her butt off and turned back to where Harry was still standing to give him a wave to let him know she was okay. But he was looking down at his phone, the lone chair he'd attempted to move abandoned at his feet. A ripple of disappointment swept through her.

He hadn't rushed over to make sure was okay, but only because he hadn't see her fall. He'd been too busy doing something work-related on his phone to even notice her. Tears sprang into her eyes and she heard her mom's voice in her head admonishing her.

No one has time for a crybaby. Winners smile through the pain.

But this was a long, emotional pain, not just a fall on her butt. Would things always be like this?

She shook her head. Of course not. Once Harry made partner, things would get better. He'd be less grouchy, have more time for her, and be more romantic. The Harry she fell in love with would come back. She just needed to wait a little longer.

Reagan ignored the murderous look Fox was sending in Harry's direction and grabbed some white chair covers. She thrust them in the boys' direction. "Here. You put these over the chairs, and I'll go behind you and tie the ribbons over them."

Fox took the covers and got to work while Wade chuckled to himself. "Hey, Fox. Remember that time we snuck in that frat party, and Milo said he was going to come in behind us and watch our backs?"

Fox groaned. "Don't remind me. Those guys were not happy about the girls talking to us instead of them."

"I was sure we were going to get the crap kicked out of us."

Reagan stopped mid-bow and turned to face them. "But you guys played rugby and were huge." Milo was still huge.

Wade made an over-the-top tough face and flexed his biceps. "We were tough, but it was us against the entire fraternity. We didn't stand a chance, no matter what sport we played."

Reagan leaned her hip against the table. "So what happened? Because I don't remember any late-night ER trips for you guys."

Fox shrugged. "Milo showed up last minute and smoothed things over with the brothers."

"Showing up out of nowhere seems to be his specialty, doesn't it?" Reagan mumbled before remembering that there was still a cameraman in the room.

After a week of having the cameras follow them around almost everywhere, it was easy to forget that they were always around, always waiting for something "exciting" to happen. And while they probably wouldn't use much of the footage from today, that didn't mean they weren't chomping at the bit for something juicy. It would be better to focus on the old Milo, the *fun* Milo, instead of talking about his absence and what it had done to everyone.

Reagan forced a pageant-worthy smile on her face and started tying bows again. "So, any other crazy stories from college? It sounds like his sisters and I missed out on some good stuff."

"There was this one time that Milo—"

"You're talking about that guy again?"

Reagan spun around to see that Harry had finally decided to grace them with his presence. His arms were crossed over his chest, and his scowl was so deep it looked painful.

"We haven't seen him in ten years." Reagan looked down to avoid the super scowl. "We're curious about him, that's all."

It had been a while since such a twisted expression of displeasure had made an appearance on Harry's face. The last time was when she'd met his great-aunt and her senator husband. Reagan had worn her nicest heels and had been half an inch taller than Harry. He'd spent the entire car ride home with a sour expression that she's since dubbed the super scowl.

"He didn't bother to tell you where he was, so he clearly doesn't care about any of you. Why spend time talking about him?" Harry glared at Fox and Wade before his eyes flicked to the camera to one side.

"Well, it's the mystery that makes it interesting, doesn't it?" Wade said, putting a hand on his chin and rubbing it with an exaggerated motion. He spun to Fox and pointed at him. "Where do *you* think he was?"

"I heard he was recruited by the FBI on a special alien-hunting unit," Fox said, his face dead serious.

Reagan bit the inside of her cheek to keep from

smiling. Wade was so goofy, and Fox played the straight man to perfection. Sienna wasn't the only performer in the wedding party.

"I think it was the CIA, and he had to infiltrate a gang of surfers," Reagan said, for the camera's benefit. "That's why he's so tan."

Fox and Wade nodded like this made perfect sense.

Harry had a tight smile, but his eyes narrowed and fixed on Reagan. Her happiness deflated. She shouldn't have mentioned Milo's body like she'd been paying attention to it. Because she hadn't.

Not much, anyway.

"Well, I'll leave you to your speculations and to finish up here. I have work to do." Harry turned to go, but then looked back over his shoulder. "Reagan, a word outside, please?"

She nodded, and he turned without looking back to see if she was behind him. He knew she'd follow, he didn't need to check.

"Just make sure you set the chairs at even intervals, and no more than four to a side." She turned to go, but Wade's arm held her back.

"Hey, it doesn't matter why he left, as long as he's back, right?"

Reagan shrugged. "Audrey seems happy, so I'm happy. I was never that close to him, not like you guys were."

"Well, he had to have loved something a crazy amount to leave his family behind. Nothing was more important to him than the Hudson girls back in the day," Wade said.

Fox nodded. "So it must have been a huge heartbreak then to bring him back here."

"He does look kind of heartbroken, doesn't he?" Wade added, and Reagan was surprised by how serious he was. Everyone could always count on Wade to lighten the mood, but to see him like this—in front of the cameras even—made Reagan stop and consider her brief interactions with Milo.

It was true, Milo's skin was tanner, and his chest somehow broader than she remembered. But underneath his hair that had grown just a little too long and into his eyes, there was a sadness. Even without knowing what had happened, Reagan felt sorry for him.

But if Milo was anything like the guy who'd left ten years ago, then he wouldn't want anyone feeling sorry for him. Really, Reagan shouldn't be feeling anything for Milo. It wasn't fair to her fiancé—her fiancé who was undoubtedly wondering why it was taking her so long to follow him outside the barn.

Reagan smoothed her hands over her "inappropriate" running shorts and walked outside.

When Harry spotted her, he shook his head in disapproval. "Took you long enough."

Her eyes went to the grass. "I was giving Wade and Fox some quick instructions on how to set up the chairs."

"That's more like it. The future Mrs. Woodly-Huntington should be bossing people around, not doing the grunt work."

Even though she disagreed, Reagan nodded. She was too worried that if she tried to speak, the tears that threatened to fall wouldn't stop. And that would send Harry off on another lecture about how she should, or shouldn't, behave in public. A lesson she learned from her mother long before Harry gave her the list of his own expectations.

Always be the perfect picture of poise and grace.

Even without the tears, Harry must have picked up on her mood because he did something that surprised her. He closed the small distance between them and pulled her in for a hug. "Come here." His hands rubbed over her back in a soothing motion as he made calming shushing sounds.

Reagan leaned into him, thankful he was finally letting some of the old Harry shine through. She buried her face into his chest and inhaled the familiar scent of his expensive cologne. This was exactly what she needed after feeling like she was nothing more than an inconvenience to Harry this whole week. She allowed a few relieved tears to fall as she wrapped her arms around his torso and pulled him close.

After a few minutes of embracing one another outside the barn, Harry leaned back and looked at Reagan. The vein in his head no longer throbbed, and there was no sign of his super scowl. His features were softer, and his expression gentle. Reagan sniffed and nodded.

"Good. Then leave the guys to the work, go back to the inn and change, and I'll see you later when you've made yourself presentable."

Reagan's shoulders drooped. The slight glimpse of the old Harry was only a tease—and it left Reagan wondering if he was still in there at all.

SEVEN

3 Days Until Dream Wedding

MILO STRUGGLED to take a deep breath when he and Audrey pulled up to the wedding boutique. Just the sight of all the white dresses in the window display were enough to bring back the painful memories of his own wedding.

Milo had been alone that day with no family or friends to help him celebrate the joyful union. Maybe if someone had been there, they would have been able to see through Kylie's lies and stopped things before they'd gone too far.

Not that he would have listened. He had been too in love to care what anyone thought. At least now he was older and wiser, and wouldn't let love blind him to someone's faults again.

"Ready?"

Milo jumped at Audrey's hand on his arm.

She gave him a gentle smile. "It's just dress shopping, I promise it won't be that bad. I've already picked out a dress, we just need the footage of someone 'shopping' with me."

He groaned. Of course she'd already have a dress three days before her wedding. Milo didn't even have to be here. This was purely for the audience at home.

"Despite all the drama of the show, I'm not a bridezilla." She widened her eyes. "At least, I don't think I am."

He laughed and shook his head. No, his sister wasn't a bridezilla. His reservations were entirely because of his past—not that he could tell Audrey about everything that had happened in Australia. He was her big, tough, older brother, and it was too embarrassing to recount the many ways he'd been brought low. She was looking at him with so much happiness, he didn't want to see the disappointment on her face when she realized how naive and weak he'd been.

He cleared his throat. "Why me? Sienna or Harper would be way better at this than me."

"Because I've missed you, and I want to take advantage of any time I get with you before you have to leave again."

Warmth spread through his chest at his sister's words. It was more than he deserved. He'd abandoned the people he loved most, and instead of being mad at him, they wanted to spend time with him.

Well, Audrey wanted to spend time with him. Sienna might not be nearly as excited. But he still had some major amends to make with Harper. And like Audrey pointed out, he would have to leave again. As much as he wanted this to be forever, he still had some things to settle in Australia before he could come home for good. The sooner he got everyone through the rest of the show successfully and got his money, the better.

Both of their heads snapped toward the store at rapid knocking on the car window.

The frowning cameraman stood outside Audrey's car pointed firmly at the two of them and then at the camera.

Audrey giggled. "I guess we'll have to finish this heart to heart later."

He sighed and followed Audrey out of the car. Milo was not about to have a heart to heart with anyone anytime soon about all of his former mistakes. Especially not on camera.

Once inside the bridal shop, they were greeted by several saleswomen with painfully fake smiles permanently attached to their faces.

The oldest of them, a woman with short black hair, stepped forward and introduced herself as the owner. She pulled Audrey into a hug, kissing both of her cheeks. "Welcome! We are so honored that you chose us to dress you on this very special occasion."

Milo snorted. Had Audrey actually been given a choice in the matter? His sister shot him a look before she pulled out of the hug to reach down and grab the owner's hand. "It's so great to be here. I can't wait to try on all of your amazing dresses."

The woman looked pleased at the compliment before turning her attention on Milo. "And is this the lucky groom?"

Milo and Audrey both choked on laughs.

"Oh, no. That's my brother, Milo."

The owner walked over to Milo and pulled him into an awkward embrace, kissing his cheeks just as she'd done with Audrey. When she pulled away, she lifted his left hand. "And not married yet."

Audrey shook her head. "Nope. Not yet."

The older woman raised her eyebrows. "Surprising. He's quite the handsome one."

Audrey laughed and punched his arm. "He'll find the right one eventually."

The older woman pulled Audrey toward a rack of dresses and started asking Audrey what style of dress she wanted.

Meanwhile, Milo fought to keep his face neutral. He didn't want the news that he was actually the first to get married to ruin Audrey's big day. With less than a week until she and Eli took vows to love one another 'til death do they part, she didn't need to hear about Milo's failed marriage.

Only Mom knew that he had married Kylie. He'd finally reached out when he'd decided once and for all to end things. His mom had been a source of strength during the messy divorce process that was finally coming to an end. The lawyer's fees were piling up faster than he could pay, and that was on top of all the debt he'd racked up while catering to Kylie's every whim for nearly a decade. Bruce's offer had come at the perfect time. Milo flopped down in a plush chair by the dressing rooms and rubbed his hand over his face. From beneath his fingers, he peeked at the owner and Audrey looking at dresses.

He leaned back in the chair, making every effort to keep his breathing even as he waited for Audrey to finish pretending she'd never seen any of them before.

How long can this possibly last? Ten minutes? An hour?

He was just starting to actually relax when he felt a gentle tap on his shoulder. Milo opened his eyes and looked up to see one of the employees who had greeted them standing over his chair.

She was young, barely over twenty, with red hair that paled in comparison to Reagan's. The woman batted her eyelashes at him. "Sorry to bother you. Can I get you some water while you wait for your sister?"

"I'm ace, thanks." Milo shook his head before closing his eyes and leaning back against the chair again.

The girl cleared her throat, and Milo cracked open an irritated eye at her. It wasn't that she was doing anything wrong necessarily, but he didn't want a girl making eyes at him just because her boss made a big production about him being single. He didn't want *any* girl making eyes at him ever again.

So why did the sparkling blue of Reagan's eyes suddenly flash through his mind?

"Does that mean yes?" Her eyebrows pulled together.

Milo realized what he'd just said. He was so tired, the Aussie slang kept slipping in.

"No, I'm fine, thanks."

He stared at her, and there must have been something in his expression to scare her off because her smile faltered.

"If you, uh, need anything, just let me know."

She scurried off, and Audrey appeared.

"Are you scaring away innocent shop girls now?" There was a playful smile on her face.

Milo lifted his brows. "Are you trying to kill me by making me come dress shopping?"

"I was only teasing you." Audrey pouted. "It was obvious that girl was interested in getting you more than a glass of water."

"And you know I'm not looking to date anyone."

"I know that," Audrey said, sitting on the arm of the chair. "I just want things to be normal again."

He sat up and let out a short, hard laugh. "Normal? What does that even mean?"

He would never be the carefree Milo his sisters remembered. And if a time came when he dated again, he wouldn't be able to provide for a girlfriend or wife the way he wanted to. Kylie and her lawyers were making sure of that.

"I mean having you here, part of the family."

He sighed and ran his hands through his hair. "Audrey, I still have a lot I need to take care of and—"

"It's fine." Audrey reached out and touched his shoulder. "I know things aren't going to be like they used to be for a long time. But will you at least help me pick out a dress?"

Milo softened a little. "Of course. Anything for my sister."

He dutifully stayed in his seat while Audrey tried on half a dozen dresses. One showed way too much skin for him to be comfortable as her older brother. Another was almost exactly the same one Kylie had worn, and it had been hard not to walk out of the bridal boutique when he'd seen Audrey in it. He reminded himself that she'd obviously save the real dress for the very end, and he wouldn't have the image of Kylie in his mind on Audrey's big day.

The rest were pretty, but not right. With a sneaky glance at his watch, Milo wondered how much more footage they'd need. He was being pestered constantly by the cameraman to get sound bites, with Australian expressions encouraged ("Strike me roan!" seemed to be everyone's favorite.)

At one point, the redheaded saleswoman brought over a glass of water with such a hopeful look on her face, Milo almost died of embarrassment for her. But through it all, he kept his cool. His sister had chosen him for this task, and even though he wasn't the right person for the job by any stretch of the imagination, he wanted to do his best for Audrey—for his entire family. And if that meant spending hours looking at wedding dresses, then so be it.

"Okay, this is the last one," Audrey yelled from the other side of the door of the dressing room.

Milo took a deep breath and sat up in his seat, a smile plastered on his face in anticipation. *This is it. Even if you hate it, this is the one she loves.*

The door opened slowly and out stepped Audrey in a simple white dress that made her look like an angel.

Milo stood up. "Wow."

Audrey walked over to the mirrors and started turning this way and that in an attempt to see the dress from every angle. "Yeah?"

He walked over to the mirrors and stood behind his sister. The fabric was light and tiny wisps of sleeves fluttered around her shoulders. Beads dotted her waistline and cascaded down in an intricate pattern. He caught her eyes in the reflection. "Audrey, you look beautiful. Eli isn't going to know what hit him when you walk down the aisle in just a couple of days."

Audrey's eyes were glassy as she held her big brother's gaze. "I want you to walk me down the aisle, Milo."

He broke eye contact and took a couple of steps away, keeping his back to her. "I can't. I'm not Dad."

He felt, rather than saw, Audrey come up behind him. "I know you're not Dad. I'm glad you're not Dad."

Milo spun around to face her. "How can you say that? I left just like he did. I'm no better than him." And just like his father, he'd left because he wanted a different life. And a woman was at the heart of it. The shame clung to him like salt from the ocean after a long day at the beach.

"You're a thousand times better." Audrey tilted her head as she looked up at him. "You came back."

He wasn't sure what he had done to earn such unwavering devotion from Audrey, but he knew it would be foolish to waste this gift and disappoint her. Milo nodded. "Okay."

"Okay, you'll do it?" She looked up at him expectantly.

He felt a corner of his mouth lift into a smile. "I'd be honored."

EIGHT

3 Days Until Dream Wedding

AFTER THE EMBARRASSMENT of the barn, the rest of the day didn't go any better for Reagan. Harry kept finding things to criticize her about, from the way she flipped her hair during their joint interview on camera, to the way she held her spoon at dinner. When it came time for everyone to turn in for the night, Reagan was exhausted but couldn't sleep.

So in the middle of the night, in her 5k shirt and a pair of flannel pajamas, she walked down to the dining room in hopes of finding a snack. She'd been paying attention to what she ate that week, in anticipation of the wedding feast, but after a day like today, she needed a treat. Reagan crept down the quiet halls, careful to keep her eyes and ears open for a cameraman.

Fortunately, she didn't see any.

Unfortunately, she didn't find anything to eat when she got to the dining room.

At least, not immediately. The lights were turned off, and Reagan was too afraid to turn them on, not wanting to alert anyone to her presence. By the trickle of moonlight filtering through the large windows of the dining room, she searched until her eyes found a small paper bag on one of the tables. She hurried over, opened it up and—

Someone cleared their throat behind her.

She jumped and let out a little yelp.

"Reagan?"

She turned and narrowed her eyes to see better in the darkness, but it was unnecessary. She recognized the voice of the hulking figure standing in the doorway. "Milo."

He took a step toward her. "What are you doing?"

"I couldn't sleep." She lifted a single shoulder.

"So you decided to steal the bikkies Marcey left out for me?"

Reagan looked down at the bag in her hands, and as her eyes better adjusted to the darkness, she could make out Milo's name written on it with black marker.

"Bikkies?"

"Sorry, cookies. I'm so tired I don't even know where I am half the time."

"Marcey left cookies for you?" She tried to ignore the way her heart ached at the thought of another woman making him baked goods, even if that was technically Marcey's job. "Marcey doesn't like any of us. What did you do to get on her good side?"

Milo chuckled. "I've worked for my fair share of demanding chefs. I know how to talk to them."

Reagan's ears perked up at this. At last, a clue of what the mysterious Milo had been up to.

"So you've been working in restaurants down under?"

A glimmer of a smile passed across his face. "Among other things."

Reagan waited to see if there'd be more, but Milo just stood there with his giant arms folded across his wide chest.

Stop thinking about his arms.

"Uh, so she made you a snack?"

"I told her I wouldn't be able to make it to dinner, and she insisted that I have something to eat. I didn't realize her idea of a late-night snack was cookies."

"Why weren't you at dinner?" All thoughts of her own hunger had vanished. Instead, Reagan found herself starving for information about him. Even if it was just to know he had skipped dinner to pump some iron at the hotel gym.

"I had some calls to make. Time zones are tricky."

"Is that why you never called your sisters?" Reagan slapped her hands over her mouth the second the words passed through her lips. "I'm sorry. That was rude." Her shoulders tensed in preparation for the lecture that Harry and her mother usually gave her when she let something like that slip.

But instead of listing the reasons a proper young lady should be polite and kind, Milo laughed. "You don't sugar coat it, do you?"

Reagan's eyebrows pulled together. "You're not mad?"

"Should I be?" He took a seat at the table and dug into the bag of cookies. He pulled one out then held it out to her. "Want one?"

With shaking legs, Reagan took the seat next to him. Instead of reaching for the bag like she really wanted to, she sat on her trembling hands. "Most people don't appreciate my more, ah, blunt comments."

Milo crunched into a cookie and closed his eyes briefly. "Oh man these are good. Who doesn't appreciate your honesty? Audrey?"

Reagan shook her head and bit her lip. "My mom. And…" She looked down.

"Your fiancé?"

Reagan looked up and saw a frown on Milo's face. She rushed to explain. "I didn't grow up with much, and my mom always wanted more for me. Harry is that more. And in his world, you don't go around saying the first thing that pops into your head to everyone you meet."

She'd said as much to Audrey and her sisters over the years when they'd commented on Harry's high expectations for her. But they'd never known how hard it had been to grow up with nothing. They'd never had the pressure from their mom to get the best that was out there, or to be that perfect beauty queen on stage and off. Instead, they'd had the supportive Mrs. Hudson as a mom. Reagan had been blown away to learn Harper had gotten a loan from her mom to start her business when all Reagan could hope for was a "not bad" when she walked out the door in a new dress and perfectly done makeup. Even her marketing business didn't seem to make her mom proud. She called it her "hobby" and assumed she'd give it up when she got married. So did Harry.

"I can't go back to nothing," she said. "I'm willing to do whatever it takes to make sure of that."

Milo nodded. "I get that."

"You do?" Reagan blinked in surprise.

"People will do anything when they're desperate."

Reagan opened her mouth to ask what he meant, but a bang in the hallway interrupted her.

"The cameras!" Reagan looked at Milo, whose eyes were as wide as hers.

"Let's go outside." He stood up and waved a hand.

Heart pounding, she stood up and made her way around the table to follow him to the door. He stuck his head out and waved a hand to let her know it was okay. She slipped out into the hallway and peered through the darkness at his towering body.

Halfway down the hall, he turned and looked back. He stopped so suddenly, she ran right into him.

"What are you doing?" she whispered.

"Just making sure you were there behind me." He reached down and squeezed her hand.

As if her heart wasn't pounding fast enough already, the contact of his skin on hers sent it into overdrive. Without a word, she followed him out the front door and into the night air.

They walked quietly down the path and through the trees until they made it to the barn. Reagan hadn't been out there since her disastrous attempt to help Fox and Wade make it the perfect place for the wedding reception.

Milo finally let go of her hand, and with the loss of contact came a chill that had nothing to do with the temperature—and everything to do with missing that connection. He walked inside, and when he looked back with a smile, Reagan followed.

There was a thump and a soft curse. "I can't see anything in here. Can you?"

Reagan squinted her eyes, but without the moon and

the lamps that lined the trails on the inn's property, it was hard to make anything out. "No, but I think there's a light switch on this wall over here."

She pulled out her phone to light the way, but Milo stopped her. "Wait. I see a plug."

Suddenly, the barn was illuminated by dozens of hanging lights above their heads. Reagan didn't know if Fox and Wade were responsible for the lighting, or if it was done by the crew of *Wedding Games*, but the effect was almost more than she could bear.

It was the most romantic setting she'd ever seen.

And she wasn't thinking about Harry.

Which, on the scale of behavior unbecoming to a nice young lady of good breeding, was right around the "puking on your future grandmother-in-law" level. She was engaged. Milo was her best friend's brother. A romantic rendezvous in the barn should be the furthest thing from her mind.

This is simply two hungry people escaping the cameras to enjoy some cookies in peace.

"The cookies." Her voice rang high up in the rafters of the barn.

Milo's head jerked around. "What?" He'd been running his hands over the bows on the backs of the chairs.

"Do you still have the cookies?" Reagan asked at a more normal volume.

Milo's lips quirked up in a half smile, and he shook the small paper bag. "Yeah, I have *my* cookies."

"Oh, so now they're your cookies?" She put a hand on her hip.

"Well I don't see your name on the bag." His grin

widened, and her knees began to quiver. *Why is he so dang cute?*

"You were going on and on about how good they are. I think I'd like to try one." This was not flirting. Definitely not. This was satisfying her middle of the night snack craving, nothing more.

Milo pulled out a chair. "Do you want to sit down?"

She nodded, grateful that he didn't seem to notice her trembling legs. Once she was seated, Milo took the chair across from her, reached his hand in the bag, and pulled out a giant cookie. "Here."

Reagan went to grab it, but at the last minute, he pulled his hand back.

She stuck out her lower lip and let out a whimper.

"Sorry, I don't know why I did that." A corner of his mouth lifted into a playful grin. "Here."

He held out the cookie once more, but Reagan didn't immediately go for it. He'd teased her relentlessly back in college. Even though it had been years since they'd goofed off together, it felt natural to do so. She looked at Milo through narrowed eyes trying to gauge whether or not he was going to pull a Lucy-with-a-football move and take it back again.

Milo extended his hand out further. "Fair dinkum. Take it."

Reagan reached out again, and at the very last second, Milo pulled his hand back for a second time.

She huffed, and his smile grew.

So this was how he wanted to play it? She lifted up in her seat to snatch the cookie from his hand, lunging forward across the table. She grabbed it, and there was a sharp current of electricity through her hand when her fingers brushed his. She jerked back quickly, knocking over one of the sample centerpieces the florist had sent over earlier in the process. It was a small glass vase with white roses in it. And while the vase didn't break, the water and flowers went everywhere.

"Oh, no." She dropped the cookie, jumped to her feet, and quickly started trying to set things right. She dabbed uselessly at the water spilling onto the tablecloth, while simultaneously gathering the flowers that were scattered across the table.

"Reagan."

"I'm so sorry. I didn't mean to bump it." She set the vase upright and quickly stuck the flowers back inside.

"Reagan."

"I need to find a towel." She started to move away from the table to search for a way to wipe the water up, but two strong hands grabbed her and held her in place.

She slowly dragged her gaze up to Milo's face, but instead of seeing a scowl, she saw concern in his expression.

"Are you okay? Did you get hurt?"

"No." She shook her head, which was slowly heating up thanks to his hands on her shoulders. "But the mess. If I had been acting properly—"

"Acting properly?" He let out a bark of a laugh that lacked warmth and dropped his hands from her shoulders. "What does that even mean? You knocked over a vase and some water spilled on the table. Big deal. In Australia I couldn't even—" He inhaled sharply and shook his head. "Knocking over a vase is not a big deal."

"I know that." She fidgeted with the hem of her t-shirt. "But Harry doesn't like it when I embarrass him."

Milo walked around the table so that he was

standing in front of her. "How is that embarrassing? We were playing around, and it was an accident."

"But lawyers' wives don't act that way. A Woodly-Huntington wife especially. She behaves properly at all times. She doesn't have a job that takes her away from her husband. She makes sure things run smoothly at all times."

"I'm pretty sure lots of women these days have jobs and husbands."

Reagan shook her head. "It's fine. I'll have too much else to do with the wedding and moving to keep my business running too. Then there will be kids and—"

"You run your own business?" Milo's eyebrows had disappeared beneath the long hair that hung on his forehead. "When did that happen?"

Reagan felt heat creep across her cheeks. "It's not a big deal. Just something that kind of fell into my lap after college."

"So you've been doing this for years and will just give it up?"

"I want to be his wife more than anything." Reagan hated how soft her voice had gotten. It was like she was trying to convince herself.

"You're not his wife. Not yet."

"Maybe not ever." Her eyes widened, and she covered her mouth with her hands.

Milo's brows lowered. "What does that mean?"

"Nothing." She hadn't meant to say the words. Even Audrey didn't know about her recent doubts concerning Harry. There was something that felt so permanent about actually saying them out loud. So why could she say it to Milo, the undeniably attractive older brother of her best friend? A glance at his face gave her the answer. She had never felt safer with anyone in her life.

And that scared the living daylights out of her.

The silence was heavy between them for several moments, yet neither of them moved. Eventually, Milo spoke.

"Does he not want to marry you?" He looked down then back up at her. "Or do you not want to marry him?"

She shook her head. "Him. Me. I don't know. He keeps pushing back the date and instead of getting upset like I know I should, I feel..." She took a deep breath. "I feel relieved."

That was more than anyone in the world knew about Reagan. But she kept the whole truth to herself. She knew that he kept putting it off because she wasn't good enough for him. She was relieved to put off the day when she'd be tied to the one person who made her feel both the best and the worst about herself.

Except, in the past twenty-four hours, Milo had made her feel things she'd almost forgotten. How it felt to be silly and listened to and...happy. It was all much too confusing to be sorted through right now.

"If that show pony doesn't want to marry you, he's an idiot."

She stepped away from him, and threw her hands up. "I can't have this conversation. Not now. Not with you."

Hurt flashed across Milo's face.

"I'm sorry. I'm just tired, and I think I need to think about some things."

He nodded. "Okay. Can I at least walk you back to the inn to make sure you get there safely?"

Reagan's breath caught in her chest. She couldn't remember the last time Harry wanted to make sure she got somewhere safely. She didn't deserve care and attention like that, but looking into Milo's eyes, she couldn't find it in herself to refuse. "Yeah, okay."

The two of them walked in silence back to the inn, the late-night snack long-forgotten. When they got to the inn, they went their separate ways to their separate rooms. But not before Milo said, "I hope you can figure everything out," leaving Reagan more confused than ever.

NINE

2 Days Until Dream Wedding

REAGAN'S FACE haunted Milo's dreams that night, and it was all because of a cookie.

He spent the rest of the night in long stretches of restlessness as he overanalyzed every interaction he'd seen between Reagan and Harry. Eventually he'd doze off, and he'd dreamt of Reagan's smiling face when they'd been flirting—no not flirting, goofing off.

Milo knew better than to mess with someone else's girl. Even if she was with the wrong guy. And Reagan was absolutely with the wrong guy.

Seeing the way she freaked out about a spilled vase was all the confirmation Milo needed for the suspicions he'd had since first meeting Reagan's fiancé.

Milo knew that response better than he would like to admit. It wasn't the cowering that came from physical abuse—though so help that puny lawyer if Milo ever found out that Harry had actually hit Reagan. No, it was the insecurity and feeling like everything was your fault that was so familiar to Milo. It was the feeling that you were trapped in a relationship that was psychologically abusive.

Milo knew it well because he'd been a slave to Kylie for ten long years. Nothing had mattered to him more than her happiness, and he forgot what it meant to have his own needs and wants. When he'd finally woken up and seen what was going on, he'd been separated from everyone he might reach out to—emotionally and physically.

He did not want to see Reagan go through the same pain he had. He needed to stop it before she married a guy who only wanted her as a trophy wife, instead of loving her and cherishing her.

He had to be careful in his approach. Milo knew better than to go charging in and telling Reagan she was with the wrong guy. He would look like a crazy overprotective brother. Or even worse, a jealous guy who only wanted Reagan for himself.

The biggest problem was timing. There were only two days until the wedding. After that, everyone would be going their separate ways, and he would miss out on the chance to warn Reagan about marrying Harry.

Milo looked at the clock. It was almost time for breakfast, and he needed to make sure he was at every possible event for the *Wedding Games*. Not only to try to talk to Reagan, but also to fulfill his end of the bargain with Bruce. Milo did not want to make that guy angry when he held so much of Milo's future in his hands.

He splashed some water on his face and put on the least wrinkled shirt he could find in his luggage before heading downstairs.

Marcey raised an eyebrow at his disheveled state when he entered the dining room but didn't say a word.

He gave her a weak smile and a mumbled thanks for the cookies before going through the buffet line. Milo grabbed a biscuit and a small pat of butter, afraid that anything more than that would turn his stomach.

Careful to avoid eye contact with Reagan or Harry, Milo walked to the table where Eli, Wade, and Fox were already finishing up their breakfast.

"Whoa, dude. You look like crap," Eli said as he shoveled a bite of egg into his mouth.

"Thanks, mate."

"Are you okay?" Fox asked. "You weren't at dinner, and then you show up to breakfast looking like you spent the night cage-fighting."

Wade chuckled from beside him.

"I promise it was nothing exciting like that. I'm just still adjusting to the time change is all. It's like midnight in Australia right now."

"But still, you look like you had a rough night." Fox shrugged. "Want to talk about it?"

Milo shook his head. "Not really. I just want to eat brekky and get through this day."

"Okay." Eli lifted his hands. "We're just worried about you. Your sisters weren't the only people you left behind when you moved. And you seem...different. We care about you."

Milo was torn between wanting to cry and wanting to roll his eyes, so he settled on throwing a piece of his biscuit at Eli, which made the guys laugh and shifted the mood. The rest of breakfast was spent discussing the latest in local sports.

Man, he'd missed all the football talk. Aussie rules just weren't the same as good ol' American football.

And speaking of missing things, Marcey's biscuits

were amazing. He still remembered his disappointment at finding out "biscuits" in Australia meant cookies and not the delicious soft bread he was used to.

Milo was just about to go get another helping, this time with proper gravy, but Reagan stood up, so he stayed in his seat. He watched her carefully, ignoring the way his heart skipped a beat at seeing her again. But he wasn't the only one watching her. Harry had just appeared, and his eyes followed Reagan like a predator. A predator with a giant scowl on his face as if his prey wasn't to his liking. As if Reagan was prey.

"What time do we need to be ready today?" He turned to Fox, who shrugged.

"I think they said nine."

It was just past seven thirty. "Perfect, we have time for a run."

"Dude, you should be taking a nap, not a run." Wade shook his head. "I've seen a geriatric sloth with more energy than you."

"Guys, please? I need this."

Wade and Fox exchanged a look, then nodded in unison.

"Let's meet outside in ten."

―――――

A NAP WOULD HAVE BEEN A BETTER idea, thought Milo miserably as he huffed and puffed through the second mile. They were on a trail through the forest that surrounded the inn. The second the deep pine scent filled his lungs, Milo felt the tension in his shoulders relax the tiniest bit. Unfortunately, the rest of his body didn't get the memo.

"You doing okay?" Wade asked, barely out of breath.

"It's been a while since I had to run after being up all night," Milo said between gulps of air. "Besides, this is a higher elevation than I'm used to."

"Well, you look like you're in good shape," said Fox, also without needing to pause for air. He jumped over a tree root effortlessly.

"Thanks."

The three men continued another few minutes before Milo slowed his pace. His goal, after all, hadn't really been the workout, even if he clearly needed it. He wanted to know more about Harry.

"Let's turn around and slow down a little," he said. The other two instantly matched his shorter stride. When Milo felt like he could talk without gasping, he dove right in. "So what's up with this Harry bloke?"

Fox and Wade both frowned.

"What?" asked Fox.

Milo shrugged, and they separated for a few seconds as they ran around a large group of trees in the middle of the path. "Reagan used to be so goofy in college. Just wondering how she ended up with someone so…" He considered the best word for the situation, but all his mind could come up with were Australian insults. "Serious."

Wade snorted. "Seriously a jerk you mean."

Milo's heart soared, relieved he wasn't the only one who had issues with Harry.

"And none of you have said anything to her?"

"Of course we have," Fox said, his voice harsh. "She's like a sister to us. We hate seeing her like this. She's so smart. Did you know she's been running her own marketing consulting business for years? But she still takes crap from Harry, and it makes us crazy."

"Reagan is stubborn," added Wade wiping sweat from his face with the end of his shirt. "Once she's made up her mind, she won't change it. Remind you of anyone?" He was grinning, and Milo tried to smile back, but his heart wasn't in it.

She'd said as much last night, that she felt like this was her only option. Milo had to figure out a way to show her life would be better without the mind games and the constant feelings of not being enough.

"So I'm not the only one who wants to punch the drongo?"

"Drongo?" Wade laughed. "I don't know what that means, but I'm sure that's what he is. And Fox almost socked him last week."

Milo turned his head and almost tripped over a fallen branch. "What?"

Fox shrugged. "He totally deserved it, but I couldn't do that to Audrey. Not on camera. She was there for me when I needed it—Eli and Reagan too—and I've been trying to make sure this whole reality show thing doesn't blow up in her face. It's been so stressful for everyone."

"Yeah but some good has come of it." Wade nudged Fox and almost pushed him off the path into the trees. "Sienna is a total hot—" He glanced at Milo and cleared his throat. "I mean, she is a sweet and very lovely young lady."

"And she shouldn't be dating until she's forty," Milo mumbled.

"Look, it's not like I'm going to ask your permission when you were gone for so long." Fox's voice was harsh again. "She's a grown woman and doesn't need anyone's approval."

Grown woman? Hearing his buddy talk about Milo's *baby* sister like that made him want to stuff his ears with cotton.

Not to mention the way Fox had said it. It was a tough blow, but not entirely undeserved.

He'd met these guys when they were freshmen recruits for the rugby team, and they'd looked up to him not just as the captain, but also as a mentor. They'd shared their problems with girls and teachers with him, along with the rest of the team. But he'd never been as open with them, or with anyone really. He'd always had to be the strong one, the one with all the answers. That's what his sisters had needed from him when their dad left, so it was all he knew how to do.

He knew if he'd shared more, let others see his weaknesses, the whole Kylie situation would never have happened. Then he would have been there for Fox when he'd needed it. He wasn't about to ask for details, but he could see the scars of past pain in the younger man's eyes.

Now it was Reagan who needed him, and he wasn't about to let anything or anyone stop him from protecting her.

"I know Sienna can take care of herself," said Milo, as they neared the inn. "But I think Reagan could use some help."

"We've tried." Wade shook his head. "She won't listen to anyone. Not even a big brother."

Milo caught sight of Reagan running out of the inn's front door, with tears streaming down her face. When his heart contracted at the sight of her in pain, he knew he should admit to the guys that his feelings were way beyond the point of brotherly affection. But old habits were hard to break, and there was still some repair work to be done with the guys before they'd see him as anything other than just another threat to Reagan. And maybe he was. He'd be leaving in a few days. There wasn't much chance of anything happening. Even if he could convince her to break up with Harry, that didn't mean she'd want Milo.

As he watched Reagan put her hands over her face and sink to the ground, something clicked into place. It didn't matter what happened to Milo, as long as she would be safe.

TEN

2 Days Until Dream Wedding

DESPITE ALL OF her best efforts, Reagan knew she looked terrible. She'd spent all night thinking about Harry. And Milo. And Harry. Her mind went back and forth about how she could be feeling something so intense for someone she barely knew.

The question that bothered her even more wasn't if Harry wanted to marry her, but if *she* wanted to marry *him*.

Of course she did. He was everything she'd ever dreamed of. Everything her mother wanted for her. Instead of a loveless marriage her mother had felt forced into by necessity, she'd gotten lucky and fallen for a great guy, who just happened to have the secure and stable background and future she needed. His moods were a little hard to predict, and he had high standards about her behavior, but that's what it took to get the kind of life her mother wanted for her.

But what do you *want?* whispered a voice in her head that sounded a lot like Milo. It wasn't a question she'd asked herself very often. Her wants weren't important.

It was Harry first, her mother second, her friends next, and she fell somewhere toward number nine or ten. That had gotten her where she was now: good friends, a handsome and wealthy fiancé, and a business she loved. If she had to give up one of those to keep the others, then it would have to be her business.

At that point during the night, she'd sat up straight in bed. She didn't want to give up her business. She'd worked hard to get those clients, and she managed to balance them with Harry's work events just fine. There was no reason to let that go.

Finally, she had fallen into a deep sleep, comforted by the fact that she had a plan now. She knew what she wanted, and she would tell Harry in the morning.

Unfortunately, she knew with the circles under her eyes, and her hair tied back in a low ponytail, she didn't exactly look the part of the strong, successful business-women who knew what she wanted. That was more Harper's domain. Even Sienna would play the role better than she could.

Reagan decided she'd wait until the show was over, when they were back home, before bringing it up. Harry was already stressed enough, there was no reason to make it worse.

Reagan took some fruit and yogurt from the buffet and sat down across from Audrey, Harper, and Sienna. "What's the plan today?" She took a bite of pineapple.

"I think the guys are headed to the bakery to pick the cake." Audrey stuck out her lower lip, but Sienna was grinning.

"I still don't think it's fair the guys won because of Fox's song," Harper said. "The girls should have gotten a chance to sing another one too."

"I thought it was great," said Sienna, and she blew a kiss over Reagan's shoulder.

Reagan turned just in time to see Fox wink at Sienna. He was sitting with Wade and Milo, who both looked over at the girls' table to see what the commotion was about. Milo's eyes met Reagan's, and she quickly turned back around, but could feel her cheeks heating up.

"Reagan, are you feeling okay?" Audrey's brow furrowed. "You don't look like you got much sleep."

"Now that you mention it, neither does Milo," said Sienna.

Reagan resisted the urge to look over her shoulder again. Not that she needed to because she'd caught a glimpse of Milo's tired eyes the first time she'd glanced over.

"Uh-oh, is something brewing there?" Audrey said wiggling her brows.

"Of course not." Reagan's cheeks grew even hotter. "We were just catching up." More like she had bared her soul to him, but no big deal.

"So you *were* with him last night." Sienna's eyes went wide. "Do I need to go have a talk with my brother about not keeping the bridesmaids awake all night with stories of kangaroos and koalas?"

Reagan shook her head but Audrey laughed. "Oh my gosh, you are blushing so much! Do you remember the huge crush you had on him freshman year?"

Of course, that would be the precise moment that Harry finally showed up to breakfast.

"A crush on who?" His voice held none of the teasing of Sienna or Audrey's.

Reagan shook her head. "No one, Audrey was just messing around."

"Who did you have a crush on freshman year, Reagan?" His eyes were narrowed to tiny slits, and he sat down with a thump next to Audrey.

"Our Intro to Art History Professor," Audrey said without so much as a flinch.

Reagan flashed her a tiny smile. "Yeah, he was like Indiana Jones and had lots of crazy stories about traveling the world."

Harry looked back and forth between the two friends. Reagan held her breath.

Finally, he nodded once and started eating.

Even her friends knew not to upset Harry. This was just how he was. Was it really any different than Sienna needing to be the star all the time or Wade and his jokes? Fox had been through a rough time, but with support, he'd gotten through it. Reagan would be there for Harry during his stressful time, even if he didn't have the easiest personality. Everyone had their quirks and preferences, but your friends loved and supported you anyway.

She got up to help herself to more breakfast, and couldn't help but take a peek at the other table where Milo was talking to the rest of the guys. She couldn't make out what they were saying, but was sure she heard something about football before they all got up.

Reagan didn't risk looking at them again, not with Harry only a few feet away, but could feel the guys' presence as they walked by her. Reagan recognized the scent of Milo's cologne and closed her eyes for just a moment to savor it.

Not that she should be able to recognize his cologne

or savor it. Startled by her reaction, her hand shook ever so slightly as she scooped up some fruit and went back to her table.

When Reagan sat down, Harry was glaring at her like she had just done a striptease on the buffet.

"So, what was this Art History Professor like?" Harry's tone was light, but Reagan could see the anger in his eyes.

Reagan took a deep breath. *I know how to handle him, how to keep him calm. That will be my job as his wife.* "Oh, you know, this leathery old guy who dressed all in linen even in winter like it was Egypt instead of the mountains."

"And you had a crush on him?"

Reagan shrugged. If she didn't make it a big deal, Harry would just drop it. "He had good stories. He'd been a lot of places."

"Like Milo?"

Reagan's stomach dropped somewhere under the table. "I don't know what you mean." She bit her lip, but that couldn't hide the trembling in her voice. "I haven't seen him in ages. Who knows where he's been."

Harry's fist slammed into the table. "Don't lie to me."

Harper smacked her hands on the table in response to Harry's display of anger. "Why do you think she's lying? Milo didn't tell any of us where he was for the past ten years. There's no way she would know where he was."

"I didn't ask your opinion," Harry practically snarled.

Sienna gasped. "Excuse me? You did not just speak to my sister that way."

The cameraman, who had been minding his own business and eating breakfast in the corner, perked up at the sound of an argument brewing at their table. If Reagan didn't act fast, things were going to end with everyone looking bad on camera.

Then Harry would really lose his temper. Yes, he was mad now, but Reagan had seen worse—usually when he lost a case that he was sure he should win. And Reagan didn't want to give Bruce any more fuel for the fire. Reagan needed to keep the focus on Audrey and her wedding—not the crazy wedding party.

"Guys, please. This isn't helping." She jerked her head to the cameraman who was adjusting the camera on his shoulder, ready to start filming.

Harper looked like she was ready to argue, but yelped when Sienna elbowed her.

"I was thinking it might be fun to do sister makeovers right now," Sienna said perfectly normal, like nothing was wrong.

Harper forced a smile. "Sounds like fun," Harper said through clenched teeth.

Audrey was the only one who looked at Reagan. "Do you want to come?"

Yes, please. I need to get out of here.

"She's a bridesmaid, not a sister," Harry said turning his head toward Reagan and wrapping a possessive arm around her shoulder. "I'm sure you can meet up later, right, sweetie?"

When Reagan didn't answer right away, he gave a squeeze.

Reagan nodded quickly. "He's right. Plus, this will give us a chance to spend some quality time together before the day's activities."

And hopefully smooth over whatever was going on right now.

Reagan watched her friends leave while a sense of dread grew heavy in her stomach. Harry and she were the only ones left in the dining room now, other than the cameraman.

Harry smiled at her, but it only made her feel more anxious about what was coming.

"Let's go for a walk, shall we?"

Reagan pressed her lips together and nodded.

They got up, but as soon as they started to leave the room, the cameraman followed.

Reagan could see the vein throbbing on Harry's forehead. He spun to face the crew member and made a motion for the cameraman to stop recording. The cameraman shook his head.

"Give me two minutes," Harry said with his best courtroom voice.

The authoritative tone made Reagan shrink into herself just a little, but it worked because the cameraman pressed a button on the camera and lowered it.

"How much do you make an hour filming?"

When the man answered, Harry snorted. "I'll pay you three times that if you let me and my lovely fiancée take a walk in privacy."

The cameraman's eyes widened at Harry's proposition, but he quickly shook his head. "Bruce said we needed to keep an eye on you no matter what."

"He what?" Harry's voice was wild, and he stopped to take a deep breath and smooth a hand over his hair. He looked down at the lanyard around the man's neck. "Look, David, I don't plan on telling him, do you?"

David shook his head.

"Good." Harry pulled out his wallet and fished some bills out of it. "Now, take this and have a much-deserved break."

David took the money and stared at it for a moment like he still wasn't sure what to do.

"I promise we won't do anything worth filming. I just want to take a romantic stroll without a camera breathing down our backs. Is that so much to ask for?"

David folded the money and shoved it in his pocket. "I think they need some footage of the inn for cut scenes. This seems like a good chance to get that."

And with that, David—the only person preventing Harry and Reagan from being alone together—walked out of the dining room.

"Come on, come to my room."

"I thought we were going to take a walk."

He pressed his lips together and shook his head. "And I thought I told you not to do anything that would embarrass us while we were here. Now, let's go before I have to pay off another member of the crew."

Harry walked quickly through the halls of Emerald Inn, while Reagan hurried to keep up. Her mind raced at the different accusations Harry might make of her, and she made a mental list of the different responses she'd give and all the best answers that would calm him down instead of provoking him further.

As much as she loved Harper and Sienna, they hadn't done her any favors with their argumentative attitudes in the dining room.

Harry didn't waste a single second once they were in his room, and the door was shut behind them.

"I want to know what's going on between you

and Milo."

Reagan felt her face heat up, and shook her head quickly. "N-nothing's going on."

Harry took a step toward her. "I will not have you make a fool of me on network television for the entire world to see. I'll ask you one more time. What's going on between you and Milo?"

Reagan straightened her shoulders and answered again, this time with more assurance. "There's nothing going on."

Harry put his back to her and cursed loudly. "Don't lie to me. I know you were with him last night. I saw you walking up to the inn together."

Reagan's breath caught in her throat. This was it. Harry had finally had enough, and was going to call things off between them. The thought was terrifying— and yet, somehow a relief at the same time.

She gave a jerky nod. "I was, but it wasn't like that. I couldn't sleep, and neither could Milo. He's my best friend's brother, shouldn't I be allowed to talk to him?"

Harry spun around. "No. In fact, I forbid you to talk to him again."

Reagan made a sound of surprise. "I can't just not talk to him. What would everyone think?"

"That you're devoted to your fiancé?"

Reagan opened her mouth to argue, to tell Harry that she was devoted to him.

But Harry waved a hand and cut her off. "Now go do something. I can't stand to look at you right now, and I need to calm down before the start of the next circus act you forced me into."

Reagan closed her mouth and left with tears in her eyes and unbearable pain in her heart.

ELEVEN

2 Days Until Dream Wedding

SOMEHOW, Milo ended up next to Harry in the van that drove them to town. He did his best to breathe deeply, into his stomach, not the shallow chest breathing that put him in panic mode. Kylie had made fun of him for doing yoga—said it wasn't a manly thing to do—but the breathing had gotten him through more than one fight with his sanity intact.

Sitting next to Harry was testing Milo's patience to the limit, however.

It started the second they got into the van.

"Why are we doing this and not Harper?" he asked. "Isn't she supposed to be the baking expert?"

"Because we won the karaoke contest," said Wade, from the seat in front of them. They were in two rows, with Eli sitting up front with the driver. Milo had Harry on one side and a cameraman on the other.

"Besides, this is her sister's wedding, she shouldn't have to worry about the cake," said Eli. "It's a lot of work, and her bakery is already under enough pressure with her being gone for ten days."

"So she gets a break, but we had to set up the barn for them?" Harry crossed his arms over his chest.

Not that Harry had helped during that task. Fox had told Milo how Harry had been too busy on his phone to pay attention to anything that had been going on. He hadn't even noticed when his fiancée had gotten hurt. Though from the looks of Reagan's face this morning, she'd been hurt by something—or someone—else. She'd run off toward the woods before the guys had gotten back to the inn, and Milo had been worrying about her ever since. At least with Harry in the car, Milo knew she was safe from him for a few hours.

Milo took another deep breath as the car slowly made its way down the mountain—too slowly.

"Do you really want to eat Harper's truffle lavender poppy seed sponge cake at the wedding?" Eli was laughing, but Harry just frowned.

"That sounds delicious, actually."

Milo turned his head to see if Harry was joking, but his face was dead serious.

"At least she has decent taste and won't just make some vanilla buttercream monstrosity to satisfy the uncultured palates of this backwoods mountain town."

"Hey." Milo spoke up for the first time. None of the other guys were from the area, but this was Milo's hometown, after all. "There's heaps of great food here."

"If you like barbecue and cornbread." Harry rolled his eyes.

"Doesn't everyone?" said Wade, who turned around in his seat to stare open mouthed at Harry.

"Those were two of the things I missed the most when I was away," Milo said. While grilled pineapple and pavlova had been nice, Milo had been craving smoked brisket ever since his plane had touched American soil. "That and chocolate chip cookies."

"Well now you can gorge yourself silly. I'm sure that's exactly what the girls will plan for the menu."

"I bet we can arrange a special meal for you if you need it, Harry." Eli somehow sounded calm and accommodating. How had Audrey picked a saint of a guy and let her best friend end up with a total demon?

Milo envied Eli's composure. But then again, Eli was getting married to the girl of his dreams in less than forty-eight hours. They could probably eat week-old pizza and have stale fruitcake for dessert, and he wouldn't notice. That kid had been totally smitten with Audrey since day one. It hadn't been easy for Milo to witness, and he'd made sure to keep an eye on them as much as possible in college, but Eli had won him over quickly, along with his other friends.

Milo had no intention of ever being won over by Harry, however. And Harry didn't even seem to care what the other guys thought of him. He had total confidence that his way was the right way, and seemed to think everyone should agree with him without question. The similarities with Kylie were becoming too hard to ignore. Milo knew he needed to do something, but what?

His first instinct was to give Harry a black eye, but Milo had already punched one guy since arriving home at Wellspring. He couldn't go around hitting everyone he didn't like, and knew it was just years of pent up frustration that needed to get out. He also knew that wasn't what Audrey would want. Bruce might want some on-camera clobbering, but Milo hadn't promised him drama. Just that he'd be here and participate in all events as planned. If tomorrow's bachelor party happened to be boxing, well then, that was a different story…

"We're here," announced Eli, pulling Milo out of his daydreams of seeing Harry knocked out cold on his back.

He shook his head. It was his own feelings of lack of control and power that made him want to lash out. No one deserved to be treated like that, even someone like Harry. Besides, it wouldn't change anything. Harry was a bully, and showing him force would just make him think that was okay. That was the last thing Milo wanted for Reagan—an angry and embarrassed Harry who needed to show someone who was boss.

The guys filed out of the van, and Milo let Harry pull ahead. He entered the bakery right behind Eli, with a look of determination that made Milo's chest tighten.

What was he up to?

"Welcome to the Sugar Fix Bakery." A smiling older man greeted them. "We're honored you picked us to make the cake for your special day."

Milo tried not to roll his eyes. It was the same speech the lady at the dress shop had given. Despite what Eli had said, Milo was sure that Harper would have been thrilled to make the wedding cake. But he and Audrey had no choice about any of the vendors. At least they got to pick some things like the flavor of cake and type of flowers. Audrey had explained the contests to Milo, and he wished he had been there for the s'mores. Even as a teenager, Harper had been creative with food, and he was so proud of what she'd built.

He'd wanted to tell her that ever since he got here, but she'd been so irritated with him, he knew it wouldn't make a difference.

"I have a great selection of six different cakes for you all to sample." The bakery owner led them to a long table in the middle of the room. Lights and cameras were already set up. Milo crossed his fingers that this would go fast.

Harry was the first to sit down and folded his hands in front of him. The look on his face reminded Milo of how serious lawyers were right before diving in with a brutal argument for their case. And apparently, this was a case Harry wanted to win.

The rest of the guys sat down, as the baker set slices of cake at each setting. "First up, we have a classic white cake with simple buttercream frosting. It's timeless, elegant, and—"

"Boring," Harry said, his fork untouched on the table.

The baker jerked back at Harry's harsh tone.

Milo shoved a piece in his mouth. "I think it's delicious."

"And it's so moist," Eli said.

Wade groaned. "Why does everyone insist on using that word to describe food?"

"Uh, because it's better than dry cake or turkey or whatever." Eli lifted his brows. "Why is it such a big deal to you?"

"Not just me. There are a ton of people who can't stand that word. It's a movement."

"Who cares how they describe it? White cake is still boring." Harry pushed the small plate away from him and looked up at the baker. "What else do you have?"

The older man's hands shook as he cleared Harry's plate. "I'll be right back with the next flavor."

As soon as he disappeared into the kitchen, Fox turned toward Harry. "What was that?"

Harry leaned back in his chair and folded his arms. "What was what?"

"That attitude."

"It wasn't an attitude." Harry straightened in his seat. "But the groomsmen only won two competitions. The least we can do is take them seriously."

Milo glanced at the kitchen to make sure the baker wasn't back. When he saw the coast was clear, he added, "There's a difference between taking it seriously and being a jerk about it."

"And here, I thought I was the only jerk," Fox said, earning him a subtle head shake from Eli.

"Just because you have a weird obsession with chocolate chip cookies and barbecue, doesn't mean that the cake has to be treated like some six-year-old's birthday cake."

Yikes. This guy was intense.

"Okay, here's the next cake." The baker reappeared with new slices on more tiny plates. "This one has a light almond flavor with a tangy orange filling."

Wade perked up. "That sounds—"

"I'm allergic to almonds," Harry said, refusing to let the baker even set down the plate this time.

The man looked at one of the crew members who stood next to the cameraman with a look of hopelessness. Unfortunately for him, Jennifer, the production assistant, just waved her hand at him to continue.

"Uh, okay. So no almond cake. That eliminates one of the others I prepared, but I think I might have another option." He forced a smile. "Give me just a minute."

Once the baker had disappeared again, Milo turned to face Harry and ground out behind clenched teeth, "What was that?"

Harry glared at him. "Well, excuse me if I don't want to go into anaphylactic shock at Eli's wedding."

"Exactly, it's *his* wedding, not yours. If that's the cake he wants, you can just abstain from eating any."

"But is it really worth the risk of more drama on their special day?"

The words were said innocently enough, but Milo could hear the challenge in them. His hands curled into fists at his side, and he was thankful that the tables covered them.

"It's fine," Eli said. "I don't really like almonds anyway. Let's see what the baker has for us next."

Didn't like almonds? Unless Eli's tastes had changed drastically in the last ten years, he was lying through is teeth to save face. Eli had eaten almonds like popcorn during rugby practice in college.

Harry flashed a triumphant grin at Milo. "See, everything is fine."

No, everything was not fine. Harry was ruining everything, and Milo couldn't just stand by and take it.

"I've got another cake for you." The old man appeared before Milo could say or do something stupid. "Not boring, no nuts."

He set plates in front of all the guys.

Harry poked his fork at the slice in front of him. "What is it?"

"Champagne flavored cake with a raspberry mousse filling, topped off with white chocolate buttercream."

KAYLA TIRRELL & DAPHNE JAMES HUFF

"Now this is more like it." Harry took a bite and made a soft sound of satisfaction. "Oh, yeah. This is it."

Milo looked at Fox with a look a annoyance, but Fox only shrugged. When he turned his gaze on Wade and Eli, he was met with equally baffled gestures from them too.

Milo took a bite. It was...actually really good. He would have never thought that champagne could make a good cake flavor, and he certainly never thought he'd agree with Harry on anything—not even cake.

Eli nodded his head. "Yeah. This is good."

"It reminds me of something Harper would dream up," Wade added.

Regret over missing out on that part of Harper's life filled every bit of Milo. He hated that Wade knew more about his sister than he did and that Harper was on speaking terms with him.

"Good." Harry dabbed at his mouth with a napkin. "Then we're done here."

Eli set down his fork slowly. "Oh, okay."

Even the cameraman and crew member seemed caught off guard at Harry's sudden proclamation.

Milo sighed as everyone filed outside the bakery. Apparently Reagan wasn't the only thing Harry felt the urge to control. Harry was the kind of guy who would never be satisfied. He would rule his wife, and one day, his children with an iron fist—everything in his path would lay in subjection to him. Reagan would be miserable for it.

And Milo would be miserable knowing he let it happen without a fight.

As they walked toward the car, he came up next to Harry. "Can I talk to you for a sec?"

Harry gave him a tight smile. "What do you want?"

Under Harry's irritated stare, Milo hesitated. But this wasn't Kylie, he reminded himself. "It's about Reagan."

One of Harry's brows lifted. "Oh?"

Milo was vaguely aware of the camera that was still filming their every move, but he refused to back down this time. "I don't like the way you're treating her."

Wade, Eli, and Fox all stopped in their tracks and turned to watch them with wide eyes.

Harry crossed his arms over his chest. "What are you talking about?"

"You like to be in control. It was pretty obvious with the cake in there." Milo hitched his thumb at the bakery.

"And everyone agreed that the champagne cake was the best."

Milo shrugged. "You're right. But cake is different than people."

Harry barked out a laugh. "Very good. Did you come up with that bit of wisdom on your own?"

Milo felt his face burn and saw Wade take a few steps toward them. Milo held up his hand at him, shook his head, and cleared his throat. "What I mean is, it's one thing to control a cake and a completely different one to control a person—the person you claim to love."

Harry pressed his lips together hard. "Are you accusing me of not loving Reagan?"

"I'm saying, she looks pretty miserable every time you're together."

"How dare—"

Now, Wade closed the distance between him and Harry, with Eli and Fox right behind him.

"Let's not lose our tempers, guys," Wade said, holding his hands up. "But Milo makes a good point. Every time I see you two together, you're always being rude to Reagan."

"I am not."

"You are," Fox said. "And the way you talk about her. It's not right."

Harry's eyes wildly passed from guy to guy, like a caged animal, before they briefly went to the camera. He closed his eyes, took a deep breath, and when he opened them again, there was a renewed calm on his face. "You're right."

"What?" Milo hadn't meant to say it out loud, but Kylie would have never admitted as much, and he was beyond shocked.

A quick glance at the other guys told Milo that he wasn't the only one surprised by Harry's reaction.

"I've been so stressed at work." Harry rubbed a hand over his face. "I need to get this promotion, and I've been taking it out on poor Reagan. Thank you for pointing it out to me."

"You're welcome?" Eli said, his brows lowered.

"I need to make it up to her before it's too late. Do you mind if we stop by the florist on the way back to the inn?"

The crew member who'd driven them to the bakery nodded.

"Great, then let's get going," Harry said cheerfully.

Milo stared in wonder at Harry's retreating form. Just how much damage had Kylie done to him? He'd known Harry for less than a week, and Milo had misjudged him completely, based on his own scarred past. Not only had Harry admitted he was wrong, but he was rushing to make things right between him and Reagan.

Milo should have been happy that his intervention worked and that Reagan was getting a chance at renewed happiness with her fiancé.

Then why did he feel so awful about it?

TWELVE

2 Days Until Dream Wedding

REAGAN CLUTCHED the dress bag to her chest. She was more excited about this than any pageant dress she'd ever worn. This was her bridesmaid's dress for her best friend's wedding. That only happened once, and she'd insisted on getting the best.

Not that Wellspring had much to offer in terms of last-minute shopping. But once the girls had agreed on a color—dusty rose—then they'd each been set free to find whatever style gown fit them best. Reagan knew exactly what made her look her amazing, but she purposely picked something simple that would let Audrey shine even brighter. This wasn't about Reagan, and she was thrilled to be out of the spotlight and in the background for once.

When she opened the door to her room, she let out a gasp. Sitting on her bed was the biggest bouquet of red roses she'd ever seen. She hung the dress carefully in the closet and ran to the bed. Roses had never been her favorite, but it was such a gorgeous arrangement she would have to reconsider that. There was a note on the front, with her name written in a familiar scrawl.

R- Sorry I've been such a grouch. You're beautiful, and I don't deserve you. -H

Tears sprang to Reagan's eyes. It had been ages since Harry had bought her flowers. It had been an almost weekly occurrence early in their relationship, but now it tended to be birthdays and anniversaries only. And even the anniversary wasn't a sure thing since he said he never knew what to celebrate—their first date, their first kiss, or the day they got engaged. Reagan liked to celebrate all of them, but she knew it was a lot to keep track of. She was happy with her birthday flowers.

The roses on the bed were twice as nice as any of those, however.

There was a knock on Reagan's door, and she turned with a smile.

"Hello! What kind of maid of honor forgets her shoes in the van?" Sienna walked in with a box in her hand. Reagan tried not to show her disappointment. She'd been hoping to thank Harry right away.

"Wow, look at those." Sienna's eyes went wide. "From Harry?"

"Who else?"

Sienna shrugged and tossed the shoebox onto the floor. Reagan quickly picked it up and laid it on the desk.

"Maybe you have a secret admirer."

"Well the note is from Harry. It says that he's sorry for how he's been acting. And—" Reagan flushed. "I'm beautiful, and he doesn't deserve me."

Sienna raised an eyebrow. "We've been telling you that for years."

"He's not always so grouchy. He's been under a lot of stress lately."

"That's what he told Fox and the other guys."

"Oh?" Reagan moved the bouquet from the bed to the desk, then to the night table. She wanted to see them as soon as she woke up in the morning.

"There was some kind of fight at the bakery apparently."

Reagan looked up in horror. "Not another fight! You and Fox gave them enough drama for two seasons worth of episodes."

Sienna laughed. "No broken plates, I promise. They had 'strong words with Harry,' according to Fox." She used air quotes to make her point.

Reagan's heart sped up. "What did they say?" She was already planning on how to fix this when she saw Harry again so he wouldn't be mad and leave like he'd been threatening to since day one.

"Not sure, but whatever it was, it worked." Sienna pointed to the flowers. "The message was apparently to be nicer to you."

"Harry is always nice to me."

Sienna raised her eyebrows.

"Okay fine, sometimes he can be a bit short with me when he's worried about work stuff."

Sienna pressed her lips together. "The boys took it upon themselves to be your big brothers and gave your intended a stern talking to."

Reagan giggled. Wade and Fox had joked about doing that with some of the guys she'd met freshman year. "Well, that was sweet of them but unnecessary. Harry and I are great."

Maybe they hadn't been a few days ago, but seeing

the effort he was making filled Reagan with hope. The charming guy she'd fallen for was still there, just a little distracted.

"I'm going to go see if the front desk has a vase I can put these in."

Sienna followed Reagan out into the hall and turned to head toward her room with a wave. Reagan hurried down the stairs, eager to put the flowers on display, and then ask Harry to come over so she could thank him.

The young woman at reception smiled at Reagan's request and made a comment about how many happy couples this show was creating. It was a nice way to think about the whole experience. Yes it was a ton of stress, and it was nerve wracking to have the cameras follow you everywhere, but so much good would come of it too. Sienna had found her match in Fox, and Harper had been able to reconnect with the guy she'd loved since forever. And in just two short sleeps, there'd be a beautiful wedding between two of her best and oldest friends.

In her happy daze, Reagan wasn't paying very close attention to where she was going. On her way toward the stairs, she bumped into someone—a big someone— and almost dropped the vase.

Reagan's face almost split in two with a smile when she realized who it was. "Milo!" Even though he hadn't seen her in so long, it was nice of him to care enough to talk to Harry. He'd been able to rekindle her relationship with her fiancé better than she had. "I wanted to thank you."

Milo's eyebrows drew together. "What did I do?"

"Just for listening to me last night and whatever you said to Harry this afternoon."

He shook his head. "I didn't do anything."

"I know Harry needed a push to get out of his grumpy mood. I'm just glad someone did it for me." Reagan stilled. Had she just said that out loud?

Milo sighed. "Reagan, he needs to hear it from you."

"Hear what?" She clutched the empty vase tightly to her chest.

"That the way he treats you isn't okay."

It felt like her entire face was on fire. "I don't know what you're talking about."

Audrey and her sisters had said similar things to Reagan over the years, so it shouldn't have come as a surprise that their big brother thought the same. But to see Milo's disapproval hurt worse than any other judgment Reagan had received. It was worse than her mother's stern disapproval of everything—everything except Harry.

"You are an intelligent, capable, beautiful woman, Reagan." Milo reached out his hands and put them on top of hers. She shifted the vase to a table along the wall, afraid she'd drop it with all the trembling his words and touch were causing her. "You know your own mind, so speak up. I won't always be there to fight your battles for you."

Her hands balled into fists at her sides. "I never asked you to fight for me. And I speak up plenty."

He raised his hands in defeat, but she kept going.

"Who do you think you are, coming in here with your warm hugs and brotherly protective instincts? Audrey and the others have been doing just fine without you. So have I. You don't know anything about us or our lives."

She took a step toward him, and he moved back.

"You left, remember? You don't get a say in how any of us run our lives. And in a few days, you'll be gone again."

"You're right." He looked down and swallowed hard, his throat moving up and down. "I haven't been here. I don't know you, but I want to help you."

His eyes burned with an intensity that Reagan had never seen in anyone outside the pageant circuit. He wanted this more than anything.

She frowned. It didn't make sense. "Why do you care?"

Milo opened his mouth and then snapped it shut.

Reagan's heart was beating a mile a minute. "Milo, why do you care?" The question came out in a shaky whisper this time instead of a stern inquiry. She'd been through too many fake friendships that blossomed during the intense preparation week of pageants to fully trust someone who said they wanted to help her. Especially with cameras around.

But in her heart, she hoped Milo was for real.

"Isn't it enough that I do?" he answered just as quietly. "There are things...things I've done I'm not proud of."

Reagan waited. The hints and teases about his past hadn't been enough for her. Was he finally going to let her in? He'd seen every part of her, from doubtful, to angry, to scared. And still, he cared. She didn't deserve that kind of attention, that kind of care.

And now she felt herself caring about him more than she should.

Milo opened his mouth again but then shook his head.

Reagan's irritation flared again. "So I tell you everything and get nothing? If this is what a selfish jerk you've turned into, I'm glad you stayed away for so long."

She grabbed the vase off the table and pushed past him up the stairs. She could feel his eyes on the back of her neck, but she didn't turn back. This was a two-way street. He couldn't just barge in and protect her without letting her in.

Reagan had just reached the top of the stairs when she heard her name and turned to see Milo racing up the steps two at a time. But she didn't stop. Instead, she quickened her steps as she neared her room, hoping she'd get there before Milo had a chance to catch up.

Wasn't it enough to have her fiancé tell her how she disappointed him all the time? And now Milo was chasing after her so he could keep telling her how she wasn't strong enough to fight her own battles.

That was so not happening.

"Reagan, wait. Please."

She dug in her pocket for her room key.

"Would you stop for just a second?"

Realizing she wasn't so lucky to escape him, Reagan spun on her heels and faced him head on. "What?"

Milo stopped short, his eyes wide and his breaths coming slightly faster than usual. He didn't speak right away.

"What's the matter? You were in such a hurry to come up here to keep lecturing me. Don't get cold feet now that you have my attention."

He blinked a few times and shook his head. "I wasn't going to lecture you, Reagan."

She let out a loud sigh and waved her hand. "Then why were you running after me?"

Milo took a step closer. "I wanted to apologize."

Now, it was Reagan's turn to be shocked. She stumbled back a step. "Apologize?"

He nodded. "You're right. It's not fair for me to know so much about you and not share about what happened with me. It's just...I'm scared to tell people the whole story. I'm afraid they'll think I'm a coward."

Reagan looked at him and took in his height, his biceps, his strong jaw. Based on his physical traits, she didn't think anyone would be calling Milo Hudson a coward. But even as Reagan thought of their few interactions here at Emerald Inn, or the random times they'd spent together in college, not a single reason to call him a coward stuck out at her.

First, he'd punched Austin, and while that was more stupid than brave, it showed he wasn't afraid to fight for those he loved. And then he'd listened to Reagan share her insecurities instead of changing the subject when things got awkward or uncomfortable. And even now, he'd apologized when he was wrong, which meant he was willing to own up to his mistakes without needing encouragement from others.

"No one would think that," she said.

"But I left all of you."

"And then you came back."

He ran a hand through his hair. "People keep giving me credit for that, but I'd never have been able to do it without this show everyone hates so much."

She took a step toward him, her feet and heart guiding her closer despite the warnings in her mind. "What does that even mean?"

"It means that things were getting bad in Australia." Milo shook his head. "No. They'd been bad for a long time, but I was stuck. I'd given up on ever seeing my sisters again until I got a phone call from Bruce Bigg about a month ago. He offered to pay my way to the states if I agreed to be on this stupid show."

Reagan felt more confused than before. "You're saying a plane ticket was the only thing that stood between you and your sisters for ten years? I would have bought a ticket ten years ago if I knew that, and your sisters would have too."

Milo rubbed both of his hands over his face. "It was more than a plane ticket. But that's not what's important right now. I just want you to know that it's not that I don't trust you. I do. It's just too hard to talk about right now."

His voice cracked with the last of his words, and Reagan felt her heart break with it.

What was it about Milo that made all of her emotions feel so intense? She'd shared more, learned more, felt more in the last two days with Milo than she had in months with Harry. Her eyes burned with the thought, and her vision became blurry as tears welled up in her eyes. Reagan fought hard to keep them from falling, but it was too much, and a single tear slipped down her cheek.

Milo reached out and wiped the moisture away, but let his fingers linger on her skin.

Reagan's gaze met Milo's and everything seemed to snap into place. She was unhappy with Harry and had been for a long time, she felt safer with Milo than she'd felt with a man for as long as she could remember, and she was pretty sure Milo was about to kiss her.

But the scariest part? She wasn't sure that she had the willpower to pull away if he did.

THIRTEEN

2 Days Until Dream Wedding

MILO PULLED BACK.

Had he just been about to kiss Reagan? Even though she was engaged? Harry wasn't the right guy for her, but Milo wasn't the kind of guy to mess around with someone else's fiancée. It wasn't right.

He cleared his throat. "I, uh...bye."

He marched down the hall as quickly as he could to put some distance between Reagan and him. As much as his mind knew it was not okay to kiss Reagan, his lips yearned to press against hers so much it hurt. And that meant he needed to go find something else to do. ASAP.

There was one place that Milo felt comfortable and knew Bruce and his cameras wouldn't be eager to follow. Marcey's kitchen had become a kind of second safe room for Milo over the past few days. Before he'd gotten his visa stuff sorted in Australia, he'd worked at a few different restaurants under the table. Kylie had hated those jobs, said it wasn't right that he had to clean up after people when he was so smart. But she hadn't been in a position to work, or so she'd said at the time, so he didn't really have much choice.

She wanted him to try to pursue business like his unfinished degree was in, but she also hated the idea of him going back to school. Too many girls, she said. It was just one of the many confusing ways Milo hadn't been enough for her, no matter what he did. He had spent years trying but had never been able to please her.

Just like Reagan with Harry.

No. Milo shook his head and turned down the hallway to the kitchen. Harry was trying to change, and he shouldn't let his own confused feelings get in the way of Reagan's happiness. That almost kiss had been the worst thing he could have done. He blamed jet lag and the emotional roller coaster of seeing his family again for the lapse in judgment.

Milo walked into the kitchen, ready to lay out his woes to the sympathetic chef, but stopped short. Harper was standing next to Marcey, their hands deep in some kind of dough.

"If you knead too much, it gets too tough." Marcey looked up, and a line formed between her two eyebrows. "If you're here to start trouble, Milo Hudson, you can leave right now."

Milo gaped and looked between the two women. A flicker of movement in his peripheral caught his eye. Austin was perched on a stool in the corner, his expression hard but nervous when he caught sight of Milo.

"I just need to escape for a few minutes." It took effort, but he could ignore the irritation Austin's face sparked in order to get a much-needed respite.

"From what?" Marcey kept kneading the dough.

Harper was avoiding his eyes.

"Everything." He ran a hand through his hair. "Reagan."

Harper didn't look up, but her hands stilled on top of the dough.

Marcey's eyes widened. "I thought you'd be trying to get closer to her, not escape her."

This wasn't exactly a conversation he wanted to have with his sister and her boyfriend, who used to work for Bruce, in the room, but Milo was desperate for help. "That's exactly why I need to escape."

He walked over to the huge refrigerator and leaned against it. But the second he relaxed into it, his tired mind caught up to what Marcey had just said. "Wait, what do you mean you thought I'd be trying to get close to her?"

Marcey cast a sideways glance at Harper, who bit her lip.

Milo fumed. "So I'm not allowed to have an opinion about your life, but you two share goss about mine?"

Harper flushed a deep red but kept her mouth shut and narrowed her eyes. Apparently this was some sort of revenge due to her anger. Great. What else had his nosy sisters noticed the past few days that he should be worried about?

"It's obvious to anyone with eyes that you like her," said Marcey. She reached under the island to pull out two pans and placed them next to their mounds of dough.

"I do not like other guys' fiancées." He leaned his head back against the fridge. It was a terrible lie, and everyone in the room knew it. "I am doing everything I can to keep them together. Harry just got her flowers because I told him to be nicer to her."

"Oh yeah, flowers totally make up for everything he's done," Harper mumbled.

"She looked happy." *Or at least she did before I almost kissed her.* "That's all that matters."

Harper narrowed her eyes again at this. "So Reagan gets to be happy, but I don't?"

Austin made a noise from his position in the corner. Milo had forgotten he was there and turned to glare at him.

"Reagan isn't my little sister," he growled in Austin's direction.

Marcey pursed her lips. "I think I'll go talk to Alex about my next wine order. Austin, do you want to help?"

He jumped up from his stool and glanced at his watch. "Harper needs to be in Audrey's room in exactly eighteen minutes to—"

Marcey waved a hand at him. "Will you just pipe down and come with me before I change my mind and revoke your kitchen privileges? Just because Harper promised to show me her secret gingerbread frosting recipe doesn't mean *you're* of any use to me."

Austin paled and followed Marcey to the door without a word. He put a hand briefly on Harper's shoulder when he passed by, and with a furtive glance at Milo, gave her the quickest peck on the cheek. Harper turned a bright shade of pink.

"And here I thought Marcey had my back." Milo watched his sister continue to work the dough. Her eyes were focused so intensely on the counter, he wasn't sure she'd even heard him.

Milo tried again. "I guess if she likes Austin, he can't be that bad."

Harper slammed the dough onto the counter. "Why are you here, Milo?"

"I told you; I needed to escape for a minute."

"No, why are you here in North Carolina? Everything was fine without you."

"I wasn't fine." Milo pushed off from the fridge and leaned against the island to look directly in Harper's eyes. "I should never have left. But I honestly thought you'd all be okay without me."

"We were."

Milo smiled sadly at the tremble in Harper's voice. She was hiding it well, but he could tell she was more hurt than angry. "I stayed away because I thought I had no choice. It took a long time to break free from Kylie."

Harper picked at the dough, smoothing it with her fingers. "Did you love her?"

"So much. At first."

Harper finally looked at him, and there were tears in her eyes. "True love doesn't last forever, I guess?"

"Of course it does." He reached out to put a hand on hers. When she didn't pull away, he continued with more force. He didn't want her to stop believing in love just because he'd been a bad judge of character. "But Kylie wasn't my true love, far from it. She was manipulative and petty and cruel. I was alone in a foreign country with no friends, no job, and with a woman whose every word, every promise, was a lie. She wouldn't let me call anyone, and she'd convinced me you didn't want to hear from me. After a while, I started to believe her."

Harper stared open mouthed at her brother. "That's awful. Why didn't you tell us all that yesterday?"

Milo buried his head in his hands. "I was embarrassed. I'm your big brother, I'm supposed to protect you, not run away and lose my sense of self due to a stupid shelia." He was aiming his words at the top of the island, and they were muffled due to his hands, but he couldn't stand to say all of this to her face. "I was a coward. You all deserve so much better."

Milo hadn't been able to tell Reagan, but he knew he had to tell Harper everything. He'd hurt her the most, and she needed to know why none of it was her fault.

When he was done, Harper was silent for so long, Milo worried she'd left. He kept his hands over his face so he wouldn't have to feel abandoned. Though, it would be only fair if she had since that's what he'd done to her.

His sister's voice, when it finally came, was soft. "Milo."

There were so many things she could be feeling right now. When he peeked through his fingers, he saw the one thing he'd been most afraid of: pity.

Harper's eyes were filled with tears. She came around the island to take him into her arms.

"You poor thing." She hugged him close, and he loved the feeling of being reunited with his sister, but hated that she now saw him as the weakling he'd been for so long.

If he had the choice between not having his sister in his life, or having her pity him, he'd choose the pity every time.

After Harper's hug reached the two minute mark, Milo pulled away.

"Thanks for not being angry anymore."

Her lips quirked up in a smile. "Oh, I'm still pissed.

You punched my boyfriend in the face. But I'm not angry that you left. I never was, not really."

Milo raised an eyebrow. "Could have fooled me."

Harper looked down. "I was angry at Dad. I was so little when he left, and you took such good care of us. It wasn't fair to expect that of you, I realize that now."

It was like a weight had lifted off of Milo's chest that he never knew he'd been carrying around. The guilt he'd had for everything he hadn't been able to do for his sisters was so heavy, he'd forgotten what it felt like without it.

"I'm sorry I couldn't be who you all needed me to be. Then or now."

Harper shook her head. "We never needed you to be anyone but our big brother."

This time, when she hugged him, it didn't feel like pity. It felt like he finally had his sister back.

"Now, what's this about getting away from Reagan?" She pulled out of the hug and gave him a glare that was eerily like their mother. "You know Harry's no good for her."

Milo sighed. "He's a total mongrel, but it's not like I'd be much better. I'm leaving in two days. I don't know when I'll be able to come back. Besides, Harry got her flowers to apologize. He seems set on changing his ways."

Harper rolled her eyes. "Flowers take what, five minutes to buy? That doesn't prove anything."

Milo shook his head. Harry had to be able to change, or Reagan would be in for a life like Milo's. And there was no way he'd be able to leave the country again if she wasn't going to be taken care of.

"I need to believe people can change. That people can forgive the worst of mistakes."

Harper's expression softened. "You're not like him."

Milo wasn't sure if she meant Harry or their dad.

With a sigh, Harper picked up her discarded pile of dough. "Marcey is going to kill me. I kneaded this to a pulp."

"What's it supposed to be?" Milo was more than happy to change the subject away from Reagan and back to the all-important topic of American food.

"Tomorrow's breakfast biscuits."

"Don't you dare mess those up! They're my favorite."

Harper laughed. "I'll do my best. But sweet treats are more my specialty."

Cakes, pastries, éclairs. Everyone had raved about Harper's concoctions since Milo arrived, and he still hadn't had a chance to see her bakery. "I'm sorry I haven't had the time to get down to Flour Girl. I hear it's amazing."

She flushed with pride. "Next visit."

Milo didn't want to make any promises he couldn't keep. "You're doing really great, apparently, for such a new business."

"Reagan's been helping me with the marketing. She's good at her job, too, so I can focus on the baking."

A pang of anger shot through Milo. "The job she's set on giving up to marry Harry."

Harper leaned back against the counter and folded her arms over her chest. "Look, I don't like the guy, but Reagan is an adult. She knows what she wants and won't stop until she has it. She's smart, she'll figure this out."

"I was smart, too, and I still ended up trapped." Milo rubbed a hand over his face.

"Maybe stay away from Reagan for a while? So she can figure it out without you interfering."

"I'm not interfering I'm—"

Harper held up a hand. "Just like you weren't interfering with Austin and me?"

Milo pursed his lips and said nothing.

"I know you want to help. I know you want to make up for all the time you were away, and it's hard to see someone you care about struggling. But this is her fight to figure out."

Reagan had said as much on the stairs. It wasn't for Milo to fight her battles for her. He'd done what he could by giving Harry a nudge in the right direction. Now he had to step back and let the chips fall.

"But if she's not going to be happy…" He sighed and closed his eyes. "I worried every day about you and Sienna and Audrey. I see now I didn't have to. You all are amazing. But Reagan is so…"

"I know." Harper gave a sad smile. "But she wouldn't be Reagan if she weren't stubborn and loyal to a fault." She gave him a light punch on the arm. "Reminds me of someone else the Hudson sisters love."

It had been a hard day, and there were another two even longer days coming. Milo couldn't fix everything, but for now, he had to be satisfied with having repaired his relationship with Harper. The rest would have to work itself out without him.

FOURTEEN

2 Days Until Dream Wedding

REAGAN WAS STILL SITTING breathless on her bed a full ten minutes after Milo had ran away...after almost kissing her.

She was relieved he'd been able to make the choice she wasn't sure she could have. She'd wanted him to kiss her, there was no getting around that. As she looked at the flowers from Harry, now prettily arranged in the vase, she waited for the crushing waves of guilt to come and take her under.

But they never came.

What came instead was her mother's voice.

Find someone stable, someone with a secure future. Your children and your children's children will thank you for it. Don't bet your life on a crush on some college dropout you can't trust.

But she did trust him. She didn't understand why, but she did. It was Milo who didn't trust her. He had so much pain, and yet only seemed focused on helping her. He wouldn't let her help him.

She knew that Milo shouldn't be her focus right now. Whatever he did or didn't do shouldn't affect her.

Things were finally looking up for her and Harry...and she had Milo to thank for it. She flopped onto the bed and covered her face with a pillow. He was inescapable. He'd come back into her life at the worst possible time but with what seemed to be the best intentions.

If his intentions were to mess with her head, that is.

Her head was telling her to be mad at him, that she shouldn't be thinking about him. But her heart was split in two. Everything had been so intense since he arrived. Even Harry's reactions seemed worse than usual. This entire reality show was messing with everyone.

She sat up, a sudden thought calming her. Yes, it was just the reality show. Once the wedding was over, and Milo was back in Australia, her life would go back to normal, except better, because Harry was finally making an effort. The flowers were the first step in getting things back on track. She loved Harry, not Milo, and that's who she was building her future with. It was like Vegas —what happens at the Emerald Inn during a reality show, *stays* at the Emerald Inn.

As if summoned by her thoughts, there was a knock on the door and Harry's voice from the other side.

"Reagan? Are you in there?"

Usually he just barged in without knocking, and Reagan was so surprised, she almost forgot to answer. "Yes, come in."

Harry walked in, his eyes down and hands in his pockets. Had she ever seen him look so dejected? She didn't think so. Harry must have been really sorry for the way he'd been acting, and her heart fluttered in her chest at the idea of things finally getting better.

Reagan jumped off the bed and threw her arms

around him. "Thank you for the flowers. They're beautiful."

When he wrapped his arms around her and pulled her close, she noticed over his shoulder there was a cameraman in the hall. It was David, the same one from that morning. Reagan wanted to say something, but didn't want to break the hug—or Harry's mood.

"I don't want to lose you, Reagan."

She smiled and breathed in his familiar scent. Who cared if the camera was here to see their embrace? It was a show about a wedding, people wanted to see a happy ending. And Reagan felt like she was finally getting hers, thanks to Milo.

There was a ringing from the hallway, and they both turned to see the cameraman grab his phone. He looked down and frowned. "I gotta go, but I think I got enough footage to make Bruce happy."

Reagan tried to ignore the pit that was forming in her stomach as David lowered his camera and walked away.

Harry dropped his arms from around Reagan and closed the door. When he turned back to the room, his eyes fell first on the bouquet, and he smiled. Then his gaze lingered on her dress hanging on the back of her closet door and a frown took over his entire face. "What is that?"

"My bridesmaid's dress." Reagan reached to take it down and held it against her. "Isn't the color gorgeous?"

He pursed his lips and shook his head. "Pink? With your red hair?"

She tried not to roll her eyes. *Boys.* "It's not pink; it's dusty rose."

"Dusty?" Harry wrinkled his nose. "You agreed to wear something called dusty?"

"It looks really good on, trust me." Reagan turned toward the bathroom. "Here, I'll show you. Wait just a minute."

Reagan's heart was thundering as she changed into the dress. His comments were softer than they usually were, and he hadn't raised his voice, but she was still nervous. She wanted to look good for him, and she knew she did in this dress. Everyone in the store had commented on what a good shade it was for all three of the bridesmaids.

Since she was already in the bathroom, Reagan took the time to reapply her lipstick and add a darker shade of eyeshadow, to give him an idea of what it would look like on the day of the wedding. With a final swipe of her brush, Reagan couldn't help but smile in the mirror. She looked amazing. There was no way he could find any fault with her dress. And he wouldn't even be looking for one, she was sure.

This was the new Harry. The Harry who apologized and hugged her like he meant it. The Harry who sent her flowers and was pleased to see she'd taken the time to get a proper vase for them.

Reagan opened the door to the bathroom with a huge smile on her face.

"Ta-da!" She stepped out and walked up and down the room with the practiced steps of a former Miss Texas.

Harry looked her up and down from his spot on the edge of her bed, and Reagan was suddenly back on stage, sweating under the critical gaze of the judges.

He crossed his arms and shook his head. "You're not wearing that."

Her breath caught. "Wh-what are you talking about?"

Harry got up and started walking around her like she was a fancy sports car he wanted to buy. "It's so plain. The flared skirt hides your hips, and it's strapless, which makes your neck look too long. If you're going to be on my arm at the wedding, you need to look your best."

"I thought it was pretty. Besides, this is Audrey's big day. Shouldn't she be the one who looks the best?"

"What do you think? She's a schoolteacher too broke to pay for her own wedding. You're soon to be a Wood-ley-Huntington."

That was the dumbest thing she'd ever heard. She almost laughed out loud, but Harry's serious expression didn't crack. He was serious. And seriously being a jerk five minutes after making a big apology. It didn't make sense. Nothing made sense.

Tears sprang to her eyes, and unlike other times, she made no effort to fight them as they spilled down her cheeks.

Harry rolled his eyes as he looked off in the distance. "Really, Reagan? It's a dress."

"It's not the dress!" She broke off in a loud sob.

He lifted his brows as he waved an expectant hand. "Let's hear it."

Reagan took a deep breath and tried to put what she was feeling into words. "I'm just so...so confused. I thought you were sorry about how you were acting. I know you got the flowers because the guys talked to you, and you finally realized how you—"

"What guys?"

Reagan sniffed. "Fox, Eli, Wade." *And Milo.* Though she didn't say his name out loud right now. Not when Harry was so mad.

"They didn't talk to me." He shook his head.

"But Sienna said—"

"Oh, yeah. Because she never lies about anything to get her way." He stroked his chin like he was considering the idea, before he stuck up a single finger. "Oh, wait. She literally made this whole show about her from the moment we got here. You don't think she'd pretend something happened if it benefited her?"

While there had been that entire fake fight with Fox, Reagan knew that had been to help Harper. There hadn't been any cameras around when Sienna came by to tell her about the guys giving Harry a stern talking to.

There *had* been a camera when Harry came by with his tail between his legs.

"But…"

Harry put his hand on her shoulder and rubbed up and down the top of her arm. "I don't need their help, or anyone's help, to know how to treat my fiancée. I was wrong to lose my temper with you. But I will not tolerate this kind of mistrust from you."

"Tolerate?" Her voice came out soft.

"Yes, Reagan, tolerate. If you're going to be my wife, you need to trust me more than your friends. You need to put me above your friends."

Reagan's first reaction was to bristle at his words. More important than her friends? But as she mulled over what he was asking, she realized he had a good point. When you married someone, you became a unit.

In sickness and in health. For better or worse. For richer or poorer. 'Til death do you part.

Those were serious vows that you didn't take with a friend. Promises between girlfriends were more like in PJs or in heels. Through movie nights or nightclubs. Through fad diets or Ben and Jerry's. 'Til life eventually caused you to drift apart.

That meant that even though Reagan couldn't see her friendship with Audrey and her sisters ending anytime soon, it was still different from marriage. And while her gut told her that Sienna was telling the truth, Reagan had to make a choice.

Friends or husband.

She took a deep breath and nodded. "You're right. And I stand by you. And I'll go see if there's any way to get a new dress."

His features softened. "That's my girl." He stepped toward her and planted a quick peck on her cheek. "Loyal and unquestioning. Just what I need."

Reagan smiled, and she shoved down the doubt creeping up her spine. Harry was getting what he needed, but so was she. The security and stability she craved were so close, and nothing was more important than that.

So she picked up her dress and walked out of the room.

FIFTEEN

2 Days Until Dream Wedding

REAGAN RUSHED through the halls looking for someone —anyone—who might be able to help her get down to the dress shop.

At this point, it wasn't an issue of getting permission from Bruce—he'd probably love the last minute drama of a dress switch—but more an issue of finding a person who was available to take time out of their schedule to drive her to the dress shop. Audrey was having a trial run with her hair, Sienna was busy helping Fox plan Eli's bachelor party, and Harper wasn't answering her phone.

Even the production staff was too busy to help. With less than forty-eight hours until Audrey and Eli tied the knot, most of the crew was spending less time following around the wedding party, and more time trying to turn the Emerald Inn and the field by the rustic barn into a picturesque backdrop for the grand finale. And not a single one of them was willing to give her the time of day. At least they were too busy to be filming as much as they had been the first few days.

She knew she should have brought her car. When she'd asked Harry if she could borrow his keys, he gave her a lame excuse about not being able to risk it getting dirty before they left.

The whole thing was maddening, and Reagan was about to lose her mind when she spotted Milo coming through the front door of the inn. He started walking in the opposite direction. Maybe that was for the best after what had happened the last time they'd seen each other. She'd just told Harry that she was by his side one-hundred percent. She didn't need the confusing thoughts that came with being near Milo.

But at the same time, he might be the only person who could help her right now.

"Milo!"

He stopped and turned in her direction. His eyes widened when he saw her.

She ignored the way her heart thumped in her chest when his eyes met hers. It was only the excitement of finally finding someone who could help.

He raced over in long, measured strides. When he got close, he reached out to touch her arm but pulled his hand back at the last second. It stayed stiff at his side. "Is everything okay?"

"It's about to be. Do you have a car?"

He slowly shook his head. "Uh, no. I just got here a couple of days ago. And—"

"Dang it." She blinked back tears. What was she going to do now? She was officially out of options.

"Why do you need a car?"

"I need to get to the dress shop."

"What's wrong with the dress? I saw Harper's, it looks really nice."

Reagan knew she shouldn't say anything. She should just tell him that the zipper broke or something. But Milo seemed to really care about making sure she and Harry were happy.

"Harry thinks it's too simple." She met Milo's incredulous stare with a lift of her chin. She would stand by Harry, no matter what. "And I agree."

Milo pursed his lips. "You're sure?"

Reagan took a deep breath and nodded. "I want Harry to be happy."

He sighed and disappointment washed across his face. "Okay, let's see if we can find you a cab or something."

"And where exactly are you taking my fiancée?" Harry's voice boomed down the hall, and it was like a bucket of ice was dumped on Reagan's head.

Milo, however, looked like he was on fire. His eyes blazed as he took in Harry's angry stride down the hall. "To get a new dress."

"I'll handle that." Harry put his arm around her shoulder and squeezed a little harder than he usually did.

"I-I thought you had some calls to make?" she said, her voice tight.

"I did, but my client had something come up. So now I get to take care of you." He flashed a tight smile that didn't reach his eyes.

Milo continued to stare at Harry for another few moments but finally turned and walked away. Reagan had the sudden wild urge to call out to him, to ask him to stay. He'd been willing to help her, and somehow she knew that Harry wasn't here to do that.

"Come with me to the safe room." His voice was a quiet rumble of anger that sent Reagan's pulse racing.

"I thought we were going to get a dress?" she said, dread pooling in her belly.

He didn't respond, but with his arm pressed tight around her shoulder, he led her to the small room where no cameras had access.

The second they were inside, he dropped his arm and stepped away from her.

"You just can't stay away from him, can you?"

Reagan gaped at him. "I was doing what you told me to do. I was getting a new dress. You wouldn't give me your keys. Everyone else is busy."

"You know, I'm getting really tired of your excuses."

Years of walking stages in tight dresses and high heels had given Reagan an ability to remain calm in very stressful situations. It was why she did so well with her clients—she could remain unruffled while they panicked whenever an event went wrong or an advertising campaign tanked. It had come in handy to deal with Harry's moods, and she was used to his shifting focus.

But this time, it was somehow too much.

For the second time in less than an hour, she started to cry. "I'm just doing what you asked. I'm getting a new dress. I want to make you happy, Harry."

He looked very unhappy at the moment, with his arms folded across his chest and the super scowl in full force.

Her sobs came even harder.

"Happy?" He dropped his arms and balled his hands into fists. "Like I could ever be happy with someone who insists on lying to me."

Reagan shook her head. "I've never lied to you."

"Bruce showed me the footage."

"What footage?" The only thing that could make Harry this mad was…The floor dropped out from under her. There'd been no one in the hallway when Milo and she had almost kissed, it wasn't possible.

Harry's face had turned slightly red, and he moved toward her. Reagan took a step back, but she was already against the door.

"You and Milo. By the stairs. You're staring at him like you're gaga over him." His eyes narrowed, and he shoved a finger into his chest. "You're supposed to look at *me* that way."

She hurried to explain. "I was thinking about you. I was talking about you. I had the vase in my hands for the flowers you got me. I just ran into Milo on the stairs. And I was fighting with him after, he made me angry." Of course Bruce would have stopped the footage before Reagan started yelling at Milo.

Harry's expression didn't change at all at this news. "I told you to stay away from him, didn't I?"

"It's a small hotel." Reagan's relief from a moment before disappeared in a poof of anxiety over Harry's continued anger. "I didn't do it on purpose. I went downstairs to look for a vase for your flowers."

"And this time you were downstairs looking for a ride to fix your dress. Does he just hang around downstairs waiting for you to walk by?"

"Am I supposed to stay in my room all the time to avoid him?"

"Yes!" Harry bellowed.

Reagan shrank back against the door, her hands clutching the dress tightly against her, like a shield.

"If there's nothing for the show, why are you even out of your room?"

"You don't have to worry. I only care about you. Everything I do is to make you happy." He always believed her before. What had this show done to him, if he couldn't trust her anymore?

"If that were true, you'd have given up your business by now."

This came out of nowhere, but it wasn't the first time he'd said it. "I was planning on cutting back on my clients soon, to get ready for the wedding."

"Well, don't bother, there won't be a wedding."

Reagan dropped her dress on the floor. The hanger made a clatter that echoed in the tiny room. "What—what do you mean, there won't be a wedding?"

"You are the most selfish person I know," he said, his eyes blazing. "I can't believe I didn't see it before now. You never think about how what you do affects me. Since the beginning of this show, I've had to constantly remind you of the proper way to act and what to wear. All while working through half the night to make up for all the time I'm losing because I'm doing the show for you. And you're going around flirting with every guy you see here."

The tears streaming down Reagan's face were quieter than the ones from earlier. Every word he said was true but not true at the same time. For the first time in all the years she'd been with Harry, she didn't know what to say to make things better. But she had to try. She couldn't let him walk out of here angry with her.

"I love you, Harry," she said, her voice a trembling whisper. "I want to marry you. I'll do anything to make you happy."

"For now, you can start by getting out of my way." He waved a hand, and she moved silently away from the door, her feet trampling on her dress on the floor.

SIXTEEN

1 Day Until Dream Wedding

IT HAD BEEN another restless night for Milo, and he knew he looked terrible at breakfast. But at least he'd resisted the temptation to check on Reagan before he came downstairs. He could have sworn he'd heard her crying when he passed by her door, and it took everything in him to not stop and knock.

That wasn't his job. And it would only make things worse for her when he just wanted her to be happy with Harry. He didn't think it was truly possible, but Reagan wanted to make her fiancé happy, and Milo had to respect that. He hoped that he hadn't caused any trouble the day before when he'd tried to help her. Harry had looked really mad.

This morning, however, Harry did look happy. Or at least, he looked calm. He was eating breakfast by himself, with one hand flying over his phone as the other shoved cereal into his mouth.

"Why would anyone get cereal when Marcey made biscuits?" Milo asked Fox as he moved in next to his friend to grab a plate.

Fox just shrugged. "Better pile it on, though, since today is the bachelor party."

"What's planned?"

A wicked grin spread across Fox's face. "You'll see. Sienna helped me since she knows this area better than me."

Milo didn't know if he should be nervous or excited about whatever they had come up with. There wasn't that much to do in Wellspring, and Asheville was fifty miles away, so unless the plan was to spend the day in the car, it would be local.

"Should I go change?"

Fox looked him up and down and shook his head. "Nah. I think jeans and a t-shirt are good."

With his mind filled with the mystery of what the day had in store for him, Milo almost missed Reagan's entry into the dining room. It looked like she wanted her entrance to go unnoticed, however, with her quick dart to Audrey's table from the door and a hoodie pulled over her head.

He pulled his eyes away as soon as he could, but not before he noticed how red her eyes were. Audrey seemed oblivious, however, and wrapped her arms around her maid of honor with an excited squeal. "I'm getting married tomorrow!" Audrey's voice echoed across the room.

"That's right, and this is the last time you'll see Eli before the big walk down the aisle tomorrow." Bruce appeared in the doorway, with Jennifer the production assistant at his side. He slapped his hands and rubbed his palms together. "Eat up, everyone, it's a busy day today. You'll need your strength for the bachelor and bachelorette parties—day and night versions."

Milo cast a worried glance in Fox's direction, who gave a reassuring shake of his head. "It's super chill tonight, I promise."

"But this morning?"

The wicked grin was back on Fox's face, and Milo groaned.

Bruce rattled off a few more instructions about meeting times and repeated "no contact between the bridesmaids and groomsmen" at least three times. The prospect of not seeing Reagan until tomorrow gave Milo a strange hollow feeling that he wasn't used to. He was relieved, however, that at least she would have a break from Harry today and could focus on Audrey.

I wish I could have a break from Harry.

Milo looked over at his table, and he was still staring at his phone with a frown on his face. Maybe he'd get pulled away for work, Milo thought hopefully, but then Harry tucked away his phone and stood up. Despite the habit everyone had taken at Milo's suggestion to bring their empty plates to the kitchen to give Marcey a hand —and get back on her good side—Harry left his dishes on the table and walked out of the room.

Meanwhile, Fox and Eli headed over to the girls' table to give their significant others a final kiss goodbye. Milo tried not to look at Reagan's reaction to Harry's quick exit, but the pain on her face was clear.

Milo really hoped the bachelor party activities during the day involved some sort of running or exercise, or Harry was in serious trouble.

No, remember what Harper said.

But Harper hadn't been on the receiving end of this kind of treatment. She didn't know what the constant doubt, the constant fear, felt like. The ups and downs of crafting all of your emotions to fit around the moods of someone else were exhausting.

Reagan is an adult. She can make her own choices.

There was nothing else he could do. Milo gave Audrey a wave as he walked out the door and into the hall. Harry was leaning against the wall, his arms folded, and his eyes on the ground. He looked sad, and there was a flicker of hope in Milo's chest. Maybe Reagan's choice had been to break things off. But if that were the case, Harry would be long gone by now.

An awkward silence stretched between the two men as they avoided eye contact and waited for the others to emerge from the dining room. After an agonizing few minutes, the other three finally joined Milo and Harry in the hall. Fox raised an eyebrow in question at Milo's furious glare in Harry's direction, but Milo shook his head. He would be good today, if it killed him.

———

UNFORTUNATELY, Fox and Sienna had planned on killing Milo—and all the rest of the guys—that morning.

The tree course and Game Center hadn't existed when Milo was a kid in Wellspring. He would have loved climbing across the trees and swinging down zip lines as a teenager. As an adult who was still more than a little exhausted from jetlag and two sleepless nights, it was like the course was designed to use every last ounce of energy Milo had.

At least Eli looked like he was having fun.

"You couldn't have done the super chill stuff in the morning and had the fun stuff at night?" Milo called out with a grunt when his hand slipped from the edge of the platform for the third time. The other three were already there, preparing to venture onto the next platform to get to a tree six meters away. No, he corrected himself, that was...twenty feet? It had taken him ages to get used to the metric system, and he wouldn't be in the states long enough to switch back.

"When I told her about your tough run the other morning, Sienna thought her big brother could use an extra workout."

Wade hooted with glee at Fox's reply. Eli was chuckling as well.

Meanwhile, Harry was stony faced and ignoring all of them, focused on the next obstacle. He'd insisted on going first in everything, and Eli had been too nice to put up a fight. "That way I can see how hard it is and do it better," he'd whispered to Milo while they were putting on their helmets and harnesses.

It was technically another competition—it wouldn't be *Wedding Games* without that element—and they were being timed on each obstacle. The winner got something special tonight, apparently, but Milo didn't waste time wondering what it would be. He was taking twice as long as the others to do everything.

By the time he finally got on the platform, only Wade was left. Even the cameraman on the ground had moved along to follow the future groom.

"I don't get it," Wade said, shaking his head. "You have more muscles than you did in college, yet you can't climb a rope?"

"The flight has me stuffed," Milo said breathlessly.

"Dude, you gotta stop with the Aussie talk, we can

barely understand you." Wade was grinning, so Milo wasn't insulted.

"It just means I'm dead tired, that's all."

"Stuffed," Wade repeated under his breath, shaking his head.

"I haven't gotten much sleep since I've been here."

Wade raised an eyebrow. "I'm assuming due to Reagan?"

"Yeah."

Wade's eyes and mouth were wide, and he gasped in mock horror.

"Not like that." Milo shoved him—gently so he didn't fall off the platform. "She's on my mind a lot, that's all. I just can't get over how awful Harry is to her. I wish I could let it go but—"

"But you have to." Wade shrugged. "We all said something to Harry. We've been saying it to her for years, I don't know what else to do. She's gotta make that decision on her own."

It was almost the same thing Harper had said. Milo sighed. It was a tough pill to swallow, but if both Harper and Wade were in agreement, then maybe he really did need to let it go.

"I still wish I could push him off one of these trees." Wade grinned.

Milo gave a short chuckle. "If only it were that easy," he said, and swung out on the rope bridge to make his way to the next tree.

An exhausting hour later, everyone had finished the course. Harry's face when he found out he'd come in second to Eli was almost worth the pain for Milo.

And there was more pain to come.

"Alright, alright, good job guys." Jason Castle was there exclusively to talk to the camera. It seemed completely unnecessary to Milo, but so did everything about this show. "Next up we have sumo wrestling inside."

Wade and Eli exchanged glances.

"Uh, I know I packed on some pounds over the winter, but none of us are exactly sumo material," Wade said.

Jason just smiled and led them back into the Game Center with a wave of his hand.

In a back room of the building, mats were spread around the floor and a giant circle that laid out in tape. To the side sat enormous...somethings. Milo couldn't quite tell what they were.

"Two at a time, you'll get into the sumo suits," Jason said and pointed at the mounds outside the ring. "First to push the other out of the circle wins."

Fox had scooted over next to Milo and whispered in his ear. "This was so we have a way to get our frustration out." He winked.

Milo's face spit into a wide grin. This was perfect. When he saw Harry move toward one suit, he ran to the other to be sure he got his chance.

But then he saw Harry's face and hesitated. He really did look sad today. If Reagan had dumped him, then would it really be fair to add salt to his wound? He'd already come in second in the obstacle course. Before Milo gave into his urge to shove Harry with all his might, he wanted to be sure.

"Reagan looked pretty upset this morning, everything okay?" Milo called out as he slipped his feet into the padded suit. He frowned when he tried to drag it up his body. Shoving anyone with any kind of accuracy wasn't going to be easy in this thing.

Harry shrugged. "Who knows. Not my problem anymore."

Milo stilled, his arm halfway into the giant sleeve. "What do you mean?"

"You don't really think I'd put up with the way she's been acting, do you?" Harry laughed, the cold sound echoing off the cement walls of the room. "I broke up with her. I can't be associated with that kind of trash."

Everything suddenly turned a violent shade of red. Milo didn't wait to finish zipping up his suit, he didn't wait for Harry to step into the ring, he just launched himself across the mats and tackled him.

He ignored the shouts of protest coming from everyone else as he fought to get the upper hand on Harry.

Milo was bigger and stronger, but he'd also been serious when he'd told Wade that he was exhausted, and the tree course hadn't helped. Just flipping Harry on his back was almost more than Milo could manage right now.

"Get off me." Harry shook his shoulders, trying to get out from under Milo.

Milo grit his teeth as he strengthened his hold. "Not until you take it back."

"What? That Reagan's trash? She is, everyone knows it, and you're the fool who wants to take my sloppy seconds." Harry stopped struggling and laughed.

That was it. Milo had told himself that he wasn't going to hit anyone else while he was on *Wedding Games*, but no one was allowed to talk about Reagan that way.

Milo pulled his arm back, and...a strong hand held it back.

Milo looked over his shoulder to see Wade's stern face. On a normal day, Milo might have been able to meet him match for match. Today, there was no way he was going to get free from Wade's grip. But that didn't mean he wasn't going to try. He tugged at his arm. "Let go."

"No," Wade answered.

"Did you hear what he called her?"

"Yeah, I did. And it's really messed up, but this is not how Eli's bachelor party is going down."

Milo could admit that Wade made an excellent point, but his fingers still itched to punch Harry in the face. He twisted some more, but Wade's grip got tighter.

"Here's what's going to happen," Wade said once Milo stopped. "I'm going to let go of your arm, and you're going to get off Harry. Then, we're going to walk away and see if we can salvage this party for Eli's sake."

A wave of guilt went through Milo. He'd been so worried about defending Reagan's honor, he didn't even consider how horrible fighting at Eli's bachelor party was. Even though this was reality TV, and there were certain things that would make this wedding different from a traditional one, it wasn't fair for Milo to ruin it.

He let out a long sigh and nodded his head.

With that, Wade let go of his arm, and Milo started to get up.

But instead of Harry getting up and walking out with his tail between his legs, he started laughing. "You really are weak, aren't you Milo? Not only did you abandon your mom and sisters, but you're too scared to fight your own battles and let your garbage friends do it for you."

Milo clenched his fists at his side. He was not going to punch Harry. He was going to be on his best behavior. He turned his head toward Eli and gave him a reassuring smile that he was going to stay on his best behavior.

But then Eli jerked his chin at Harry, giving Milo permission.

Milo smiled before he turned around and socked Harry right in the nose.

Harry staggered back and both of his hands flew to his face with a curse. When he lowered them they were free of blood but he still gave Milo a murderous stare. "Don't think you've heard the last from me. This is assault, and I will be pressing charges."

Harry stormed out, and one of the production crew raced over to Milo. "Don't worry. He can't actually press charges. There are plenty of clauses protecting the producer and the contestants. So please just keep going and don't worry about what just happened."

And just as quickly as he came over, he was out of the way and back to the side of the room.

Even though the groom had given his blessing to what just occurred, Milo still felt horrible for ruining the bachelor party. He walked the few feet to where Eli was still standing. "I'm sorry, man."

"Don't be." Eli slapped his arm. "Believe me, he had it coming. You've only had to deal with him for a couple of days. We've been stuck here with him for a week and a half."

Milo snorted.

"But…"

Milo sobered. There was always a but.

"Harry's not Kylie."

All the breath left Milo's lungs at the mention of her name. Eli knew that Kylie was horrible, but he didn't know the details. He didn't know that they were the same in so many ways.

"Hitting him isn't going to change anything. It's not going to make you feel better for more than a minute. And it's not going to make Reagan feel better either."

Milo shook his head. "I wasn't doing it for Reagan."

Eli raised a brow.

"Fine. I may have been trying to fix things for her too."

Eli gave him a sad smile. "You can't fix everything. You need to know that."

Milo nodded.

"And you also need to know that just because you started a fight with Harry, doesn't mean you get to pass on this part of the party." Wade walked over with a smile. "So suit up in the fat man costume and get your butt in the ring. Because I'm going to love knocking you over."

"In your dreams," Milo fired back, even though he knew he didn't stand a chance against his friend. At least things would be a lot more fun now.

SEVENTEEN

1 Day Until Dream Wedding

REAGAN WASN'T sure what was harder—pretending her heart wasn't broken, or pretending she actually cared who won the toilet paper dress contest.

She had been looking forward to the bachelorette party from day one. Everything had been planned down to the last detail: the silly games in the morning, the spa afternoon, the movie night in their PJs. But Reagan's heart just wasn't in it. It was laying somewhere in her room upstairs, shattered in a thousand pieces.

"Reagan come tie this off for me." Audrey held up a skirt she'd managed to weave from three different rolls of toilet paper. It was actually pretty creative, and Reagan was thrilled to see her looking so happy.

With a smile that took every single ounce of energy she had, Reagan got up from her seat and positioned herself behind her best friend. They were in a meeting room that the crew had transformed to look like a fancy bedroom. Toilet paper rolls were scattered everywhere, along with papers filled with M.A.S.H. and strings of beads from their earlier games. There were only the four of them, so nothing really took that long. At this rate, by noon they'd have run out of things to do, even with the production assistant asking for three takes of everything.

"I'm sorry it's not quite the same as if I'd been able to host in my apartment," Reagan said softly as she tied the skirt as gently as possible. She held her breath when Audrey twirled, but it stayed in place. "We could have invited all your teacher friends, and the cousins and everyone."

"They'll be here tomorrow," Audrey said with a wave of her hand. "I didn't get married to play games. I'm getting married to spend the rest of my life with Eli."

Then why did you agree to this crazy plan? Reagan wanted to ask. *It's ruined everything.*

No, that wasn't fair. It wasn't Audrey's fault that Harry had finally realized Reagan wasn't good enough for him.

"Are you doing okay?" Audrey put a hand on her shoulder. She'd asked the same thing when Reagan had come into the dining room that morning with red, puffy eyes, but Reagan had just said she'd been writing the maid of honor's speech and had gotten teary. Which hadn't been entirely a lie—she had written it the day before—but the last thing she wanted was to ruin these last twenty-four hours for Audrey.

Reagan's mother would have had something to say about ruining her best friend's wedding with her troubles. *Don't worry others with your problems. You're a big girl, figure it out on your own.*

Reagan nodded. "Of course."

"But are you really?" Sienna asked from across the

room. She was tying toilet paper bows in Harper's hair. Both women's faces were etched with concern.

"Yes." Now all three of them were staring at her, their eyes wide and turned down with worry. She wanted to say something so badly, but what kind of friend brings up her breakup at a bachelorette party? Plus their questions meant the cameras were focused right on her. If she was going to confide in someone, it wouldn't be like this. "But I think I could use some fresh air."

Reagan walked out of the small room, holding her breath as she waited to see if a cameraman would follow her. When no one stepped out the door behind her, Reagan let out a relieved sigh.

She could feel the tears coming again, and as much as she loved the Hudson sisters, she didn't think she could handle their looks of pity for a minute longer. And that was without them even knowing that Harry had broken things off. Though, they'd know soon enough. Then she'd not only be dealing with the pain of the breakup but also the embarrassment of it.

Audrey was getting married to the love of her life, Sienna and Fox had met and fallen in love, and Harper and Austin had reunited and rekindled their relationship. And instead of being paired off like everyone else, Reagan was in the middle of the worst heartache she could imagine.

It was awful. She needed a break from the warm and fuzziness of it all.

She stepped outside and took a few deep, calming breaths while she walked around the perimeter of the Emerald Inn, enjoying the fresh scent of pine and the crisp air. Reagan tried not to imagine the cruel look of

Harry's face as she walked and tried to focus more on the excitement of Audrey's big day.

But every time she truly felt joy over her best friend getting married, she was hit by a wave of sadness over her own failed relationship. Her thoughts felt like a ping-pong ball with the way it went back and forth.

Maybe another lap around the property will help.

She was just passing back by the front door when she saw Harry storming out to his car, suitcase in hand. Reagan didn't think, she just reacted.

"Harry!"

He stopped and turned toward her, and when he did, she could see that there was a large, purple mark under one of his eyes.

"Oh my goodness." She rushed over to him. "Are you okay?"

He pressed his lips together and shook his head. "No, I'm not okay. This entire trip has been a waste of time. And now I get to go back to work with a broken nose and a bruise like some backwoods brute, thanks to Milo."

"He didn't." Reagan groaned and reached out to touch his face.

Harry grabbed her wrist. "Don't touch me. Don't call me. Don't even think about me. I know once I'm gone, I won't think about you."

The words cut deep. "You don't mean that. Once the wedding is done, we—"

"Don't, Reagan. I'm done." He dropped her hand. "Now you and Milo can do whatever you want. You deserve each other."

Reagan opened her mouth to argue, but was surprised when nothing came out. She didn't want something with Milo, did she? Her lips tingled at the thought of their almost kiss, and she hated that she was even thinking about that while Harry stood in front of her giving his final goodbye.

"There's no fraternizing between groomsmen and bridesmaids," a woman's voice called out. Reagan and Harry both turned to see a crew member walking over. "If Bruce saw you together, he would lose his mind."

"Well, don't worry. I'm leaving, so there's no chance of us talking ever again." He looked at Reagan as he punctuated the last few words.

"What?" the woman said, her eyes wide. "Where are you going?"

"The same place I should have gone a week ago. Home. I'm done with this second-rate production." Harry turned on his heels and started walking toward his car.

"Wait, no. You can't go. What about the contract?"

He stopped long enough to pull a business card from his wallet. "Tell Bruce to have his lawyers call me."

The woman's breathing came in quick bursts. "Oh, no. This isn't good."

"Drop off the ring with my secretary by next Friday, Reagan."

With those final words, the doors shut forever on the future she'd planned. Reagan watched Harry get into his car and drive down the path toward the interstate. It was like a piece of her heart was driving off with him. She'd spent years trying to be everything he wanted, everything he needed. What was she going to do now? When his car was out of view, she turned back toward the Emerald Inn, her mother's voice echoing in her head.

There goes your last chance at happiness.

"Where are you going?" The crew member was still there. Reagan glanced at her badge. Jennifer. Sounded familiar. Was this the girl who had gotten in the middle of Harper's love story? Reagan felt a bit of fondness for the woman. Broken hearts could make you do crazy things.

Speaking of crazy, Reagan was fighting the temptation to run down the inn's long steep driveway to chase after his car. The only thing holding her back was knowing it would look completely pathetic. By some miracle, there had been no cameras to capture Harry ripping Reagan's heart out, and the only person who would see her running after him would be Jennifer, but Reagan clung to that last shred of dignity. Besides, at least Harry left, and she wouldn't have to see him again. Jennifer couldn't hide. She had to be professional with Harper, the girl who'd won the heart of Austin. Though, Reagan knew that Austin had never stopped loving Harper, and Jennifer had apparently been quite sneaky and mean, so it was hard to feel too sorry for her.

Reagan knew she was spending way too much time thinking about someone else's heartbreak, but what other choice did she have? The second she thought about the pain coursing through her veins, it threatened to overwhelm her completely. She wanted to curl up on the ground and cry. She felt empty, hopeless, and lost.

Jennifer cleared her throat, pulling Reagan out of her spiraling thoughts. She was looking at her expectantly.

Reagan shook her head to clear it. She hadn't answered Jennifer's question. Where was she going? Nowhere. "Inside."

"No, I need you to call Harry and have him come back."

Reagan gave Jennifer a sad smile. "He's not coming back. There's nothing I can say or do anymore."

"But, but…"

"You're going to have to figure this one out on your own."

Reagan continued walking toward the inn, realizing how true those words were for her as well. Things were truly over with Harry this time. There would be no more flowers or apologies. This was the end. And now that the urge to run after him to beg him to take her back had passed, the only thing she wanted to do right now was go to her room, put on some comfy clothes, and eat ice cream until she couldn't anymore.

She walked through the front doors, with the mission to find a pint of Moose Tracks the only thing on her mind, but someone reached and grabbed her hand before she made it very far.

"Quick. Come with me."

It was Milo. And she did.

EIGHTEEN

1 Day Until Dream Wedding

REAGAN'S BREATH came out in quick gasps as the door of the safe room closed behind her and Milo. The quick walk down the hall to get there unnoticed was only half the reason. Once instead, Milo turned the lock. "That okay?"

Reagan nodded, unsure of how she should feel about being locked in the small room with Milo.

"I heard Harry broke off the engagement."

Another nod.

"How are you doing?"

That question was a little harder to answer.

It felt like Harry had ripped her chest open and pulled out her heart. Then stomped on it several times and put it back. She couldn't imagine how hard it would be to make it through each day with that deep ache. She didn't know how she was going to make it through Audrey's wedding tomorrow.

"I...I don't know. It hurts so much right now." Tears sprung up in the corners of her eyes.

"I know. But it won't always feel that way. I promise." He took a step closer to her in the small room. "One day you'll realize you're better off without him. "

She let out a self-deprecating laugh. "Oh, yeah. And how would you know?"

"My situation with Kylie taught me a lot about heartache."

Reagan looked up at Milo and held his gaze. In his eyes was pain that mirrored her own. Maybe he really did know what it felt like to have the person you love leave. "She broke your heart."

"It was more than breaking my heart. Mine and Kylie's situation was pretty similar to yours and Harry's."

What did that mean? Reagan was dying to know. The last time she'd pressed him about what had happened between Kylie and him, Milo had shut her down, saying it was too embarrassing. But now that Reagan had been dumped—though that word didn't feel nearly powerful enough—she had a bit of an advantage in the humiliation game.

She reached out and touched his arm. "Milo."

His eyes snapped to her hand.

"What happened with Kylie?"

He closed his eyes. "She was emotionally manipulating and controlling. Just like Harry."

Manipulating? Controlling? Reagan took a step back and shook her head. "No, Harry wasn't like that."

"Wasn't he, though?" Milo opened his eyes and stared deeply into Reagan's. "He didn't want you doing this or doing that, always dictating how you should act or what you should say. When you didn't do exactly as he wanted, he made you feel like you were inadequate."

"That was only because he's a Woodley-Huntington.

That family has incredibly high standards, and he wanted me to fit in." She paused. "Because he loved me."

"Only if you call love a desire to control you or put you down to feel good about himself. Trust me. I know what it's like to be on the receiving end of that kind of *love*." He sighed. "I was stuck in a relationship like that for almost ten years."

"Kylie controlled you the whole time you were in Australia?" The idea of anyone telling big, strong Milo what to do was baffling.

"No."

Reagan was confused. "If that wasn't it, then what are you trying to tell me?"

He scrubbed his hands over his face. "It happened long before we went to Australia. Her manipulation is how I ended up leaving my home and my family in the first place."

Reagan held her breath as she waited for him to continue.

"The first time I met Kylie was after one of our rugby games. She rushed the field after our win, and we ended up talking all night. She was a foreign exchange student who was going back home to Australia in a couple of weeks, but I liked talking to her." He shrugged. "So we decided to make the most of our time together."

Reagan completely understood that feeling. When she and Harry started dating, they'd spent every waking moment together. She didn't remember Milo dating anyone when they were in college together, but then again, he'd been a senior with his own life. And he wouldn't have shared much with his sister about his love life.

"Then she left. And though I missed her, I thought that was the last time I'd ever see her."

"But…"

"But I got a phone call a month later saying she was pregnant—and that the baby was mine."

Reagan sucked in a quick breath. "You're a dad?" Her hands reached for a shelf to support her. This was way more than she expected.

"No." He paused and looked off at the corner of the room. "But I thought I was."

"So you did the decent thing and moved down there to be with your family."

He nodded. "Yeah."

"So then, why not just tell everyone what was going on? Your sisters would have been so proud of you for wanting to be active in your child's life, considering your dad left."

"Yeah." He let out a long sigh. "But things were complicated. Or, at least, that was the excuse I kept telling myself."

"What happened?"

"I told my mom that I was leaving, and we got into a big fight."

"She knew?" she asked, eyes wide. "She knew this whole time where you were?"

"I was afraid if I told Audrey or Harper, they'd just take her side. I couldn't stand the thought of them not being supportive, so I left without saying goodbye. I don't think she wanted my sisters to know I'd left because of a girl. I didn't talk to her until about a year ago when I told her she'd been right."

"Oh, Milo." She reached out, grabbed his hand, and squeezed.

He pulled it back, and avoided making eye contact with Reagan. "Long story short, she lied about being pregnant."

Reagan's eyebrows shot up. "Who would do something like that? And why?"

Milo shrugged. "I spent years trying to answer those questions. Some people just are the way they are and nothing can change that."

Reagan let that sink in for a minute. She'd said the same thing about Harry countless times, to herself, to her friends, but as a way to defend him. Never once had it occurred to her that his unwillingness to change wasn't a sign of stability, but the exact reason she shouldn't be with him.

"So why didn't you come back when you found out she lied?"

Milo sighed and ran a hand through his hair. "By that point, it was complicated. Her dad paid a lot of money for us to get married when I was on a tourist visa. Then he bought us a house for our growing family with the condition that I'd pay him back for all of it. By the time I found out Kylie had faked the pregnancy, it was too late. I owed too much and didn't know what to do. I tried to make it work, but I couldn't find jobs that easily, and she had me convinced for a while that she'd lost the baby because of working, so she was at home all the time."

He'd started pacing around the small room, his eyes on the ground and his hands on his hips. "Then I'd get home after working two or three jobs, and she'd have a list of things to do at home, always reminding me of what I owed her dad if I ever complained. There was never time to make friends, I had no one who could help, and I didn't see what was happening. She'd tell me I was too stupid to find a real job, or that I shouldn't bother calling home because they wouldn't want to talk to such a failure.

"After a while, I just kind of gave up, you know? I accepted that that was my life. No matter what I did, I was never enough for Kylie." He stopped just long enough to meet Reagan's eyes. "Just like you were never enough for Harry."

Milo was quiet after that, his face twisted with emotion after sharing his story.

Reagan used the silence to consider everything he had just shared. Milo had been through something terrible, and she understood why he wasn't quick to share all the details. Kylie had treated him like garbage.

And that's what Harry had been doing to her all along.

Dangling a wedding in front of her, much like Kylie had dangled a family. How could Milo have resisted the chance to be a real dad, to make up for the awful one he'd had? Kylie had kept Milo from reaching out to anyone who could help. She'd made sure he was alone and dependent on her. Harry had wanted Reagan to quit her job so that she was entirely reliant on him.

"I think you're right," she said.

Milo jerked like she'd interrupted a deep train of thought. "About what?"

"About Harry being like Kylie. He was a controlling jerk who manipulated me."

Milo smiled sadly. "I'm sorry we have that in common."

"Me too," she said softly. "But at least you were strong enough to get away. I was too blind to see it and would have stayed with Harry forever if he hadn't broken things off."

"Is that what you think? That I'm strong? The only reason I'm back is because Bruce Bigg called me up one day and offered to pay most of my debt if I showed up to Audrey's reality TV wedding."

"Still. I wish I could be like you. I wish I would have been able to leave Harry."

Milo took a step toward Reagan. "You would have eventually woken up. I know it."

She shook her head. "That's the thing. I would have never seen it for myself. I needed someone to tell me what to do. Even if that someone was Harry, and it was him breaking things off. I can't remember the last time I did something for myself."

Growing up, it was always her mom telling her what to wear and how to act. Reagan had never been good enough for her mom, and those feelings of inadequacy had spilled over into her adult life. It was only fitting she'd end up with a guy who also made her feel terrible about herself. What did love without criticism even look like?

She looked up at Milo, tears filling her eyes. "What do I do?"

Milo let out a gentle laugh and pulled Reagan against his chest. She breathed in deep and listened to his heart beating against his chest as he stroked her hair. He smelled like the mountains and pine trees. "That's the great thing about being free. You get to stop and think about what *you* want to do for once."

Reagan pulled her head back just enough to look at Milo's face. "Is that what you're doing?"

He laughed again, causing his chest to rumble against hers. "The problem is that I'm not free yet. I still have to go back and sign a few more papers before I get to start living my life."

"But for all intents and purposes, you're free." She relaxed against him and found comfort with his arms surrounding her. "Have you started thinking about what you want?"

He rested his head on top of hers. "I have."

Reagan wished he would have elaborated, but he had already shared so much, and it felt unfair to push him anymore. "Do you think you'll get it?"

He took a deep breath. "Only time will tell. I'm not in a hurry, and I can be patient."

"I hope you get what you want."

"Me too." He squeezed her, and she felt a sudden flutter deep in her chest. "But I don't think you need to worry about me anymore. I think you need to find some solitude and think about what you want."

Reagan laughed and pulled out of Milo's embrace. "Oh, yeah. Because that's easy on the set of a reality TV show."

"I hear faking a stomach bug works really well." He raised a single brow making Reagan laugh again.

She wasn't sure how successful Fox pretending to be sick Audrey had been, but maybe if she was lucky, she would be able to take a little time to herself before putting on a happy face.

She never would have even been able to imagine spending time thinking about what she wanted if Milo hadn't opened up to her and shared his own experience.

KAYLA TIRRELL & DAPHNE JAMES HUFF

If it wasn't for their almost kiss, they wouldn't even be having this conversation at all. There had been so much pain today, but she felt hopeful for the first time in a long time. A lot had changed in the last few days, and there was one person responsible.

She leaned up on her tip toes and kissed Milo's cheek. "Thank you for everything."

"You're welcome." He put his hand to where her lips had pressed against his skin. "I hope you're able to figure it out."

Reagan gave him one last lingering look before she nodded and walked out of the safe room. There weren't any people or cameras as far as she could see, and she was grateful because Milo was right, she had a lot she needed to think about.

And she knew the perfect spot.

NINETEEN

The Day of the Dream Wedding

MILO HADN'T BEEN able to stop thinking about Reagan's kiss since it happened the day before. In terms of kisses, it was more platonic than anything, and yet, there was something special about it. At least it had been special to him. Not that Milo could tell Reagan how he felt about her—not when she was still feeling the pain of a very recent breakup.

But if he didn't tell her now, then he'd lose his chance.

He was going back to Australia tomorrow to close out that chapter of his life for good, and there was no telling what Reagan would be up to when he got back. He'd told her to find out what she wanted—what if that meant moving halfway across the country for a fresh start?

"Milo."

He shook his head to clear his thoughts at the sound of Eli's voice. "What?"

Wade laughed. "We were just wondering if you were going to get your head in the game any time soon. Not only are you supposed to walk your sister down the aisle in less than an hour, you're a stand-in groomsmen now that Harry is gone."

"Not that I'd call Milo a stand-in." Eli slapped his back. "I'd much rather have him at my side than Harry."

"I'll second that," Fox said.

"Admit it, you attacking him last night was just your sly way of getting the last groomsmen spot." Wade laughed.

Milo rolled his eyes. "Oh yeah. Because I'm the only one who didn't want him here. Besides, you heard the way he was talking about her."

The guys were quiet and avoided Milo's eyes. He knew exactly what they were thinking—that he only punched Harry for Reagan. "And the way he was talking about everyone. It wasn't right."

But his amendment wasn't enough to dispel the awkwardness in the room.

"So anyone know how to get this thing on?" Wade said, breaking the silence. He lifted a plastic container with a white rose boutonniere in it.

"Yeah. I can help." Milo grabbed the flower from Wade and pulled out the small pin from the back. "Hold still."

Wade chuckled. "Oh, so now you think you can give me orders? Fox is still best man, you're just third groomsman."

Milo rolled his eyes. "Do you want my help or not?"

Wade glanced over to where Eli and Fox were also trying to pin their boutonnieres to each other's suit jackets and nodded. "Fine. But if you poke me, I won't hesitate to pin you down again."

"You only got me last night because I was tired." Milo shook his head.

Wade raised his brows. "And what will be your excuse if I do it now? Too distracted with thoughts about Reagan?"

Milo's hands stilled.

"Don't worry, they didn't hear me. But even if they did, we've all noticed this thing growing between you and Reagan."

"There's not anything growing between us. I'm in the middle of a divorce. She's just broken off her engagement. This isn't a great time."

Wade shook his head. "That doesn't mean it's not there."

"If anything, it's friendship," Milo said, even as his heart yelled "liar" so loudly it was impossible to ignore.

"No, friendship is what *I* have with Reagan. What you guys have is...different," Wade said as he grabbed another rose from the table. "Now tell me how to get this thing on you."

Why did Wade think he knew what was going on between Milo and Reagan, when Milo didn't even know?

"Give me that before you poke a hole in me." Milo sighed and grabbed the boutonniere from Wade. When he finished, he turned back to Wade and asked, "So why did nothing ever happen between you two? You guys seem to get along well enough."

"We do." Wade shrugged. "But she's the kind of girl who wants marriage, kids—the whole shebang. And I don't think I'll ever settle down."

"And you think I will? I'm just getting out of a

marriage I was trapped in for ten years. I don't know that I'll ever be willing to take that leap again."

Wade reached out and squeezed Milo's shoulder. "I don't think anyone is expecting you to rush into another relationship. That's not a good idea for you or for Reagan. But if you ever did, she would be the right one for you."

Milo thought of the way he felt whenever Reagan was around. He wanted to know everything about her. He wanted to protect her. And even though it was a bad idea, he still wanted to kiss her. "Maybe, but that doesn't mean that I—"

"And"—Wade lifted his brows—"you *would* be the right guy for her. You don't see the way she lights up when you're near her because you don't know how she looks when you're not around. I doubt even she realizes it yet. But one day, you'll be perfect for each other."

Milo snorted. "Maybe."

"I've seen crazier things. Like Eli getting married on network TV, and Fox falling for an actress."

"Actor," Fox corrected.

Wade spun to face him. "Have you been eavesdropping on us this whole time? Pretty rude, don't you think?"

Fox threw the plastic container at Wade. "Don't get too excited. I don't think you're that interesting. I just heard the word actress and needed to make sure you knew the correct term."

"Because you're just so proud of your new girlfriend." Wade smirked and crossed his arms playfully across his chest.

"Careful." Milo stuck up a finger and pointed it at

Fox. "She's still my baby sister, and I'm not super comfortable with the idea of my friend dating her."

"What about another friend of yours marrying a different sister?" Eli looked down at his watch. "Because that's happening in, like, forty-five minutes, assuming Bruce doesn't have any more *fun* surprises in store for us."

Fox groaned. "I don't know that I can handle any more surprises. As it stands, I'm going to need a vacation to recover from this one."

Wade laughed. "You know, I think Sienna makes an excellent point when she compares you to an old, grumpy man. Have you ever sounded more lame?"

"Well, I think you're—"

A knock interrupted whatever Fox was going to say, and it was for the best. The back and forth between those two could have lasted all day if no one stepped in. And Bruce Bigg literally did that. He walked into the room with his usual air of authority, and Milo held his breath as he waited for the other shoe to drop.

Please don't let this be another surprise.

"Milo." He flashed his unnaturally white teeth. "Audrey is just about ready, and it's time for you to go see your sister all dressed up for her big day."

His shoulders sagged in relief. Not another contest or competition, just a brother getting to spend a few minutes with his sister before he walked her down the aisle. He turned and looked at Eli. "I guess I'll see you on the other side."

Eli gave him a smile. "Wish me luck."

"You don't need it." Milo shook his head. "You guys are perfect for each other."

"And remember what we talked about," Wade said.

Could Milo and Reagan be perfect for each other too? Unfortunately, now that Wade had put the thought in is head, Milo was in no danger of forgetting it anytime soon. He gave Wade a quick nod just before following Bruce out into the hallway.

"I must say, bringing you in for the show was one of my best ideas," Bruce said over his shoulder as he led Milo to the bride's room. A cameraman followed close behind them.

Milo kept his mouth shut and focused on putting one foot in front of the other instead. He was nervous to be alone with Bruce, nervous to have the task of giving Audrey away, and nervous about seeing Reagan again after their talk the night before.

He needed to keep it together rather than allow himself to be baited by the show's producer.

"I wasn't sure after Sienna caused so much unnecessary drama. But I like the tension between you and Harry. And also between you and Reagan." He paused and looked over his shoulder. "She looks beautiful, by the way."

Milo gave Bruce a shaky smile.

A flash of disappointment appeared on Bruce's face for the briefest moment before he turned his head and started walking again. "Anyway, you'll walk Audrey down the aisle, and then take your place at the end of Eli's groomsmen. Understood?"

"Yeah."

Bruce stopped. "Good, then I'll let you find the rest of the way to the bride's room. It's just around the corner."

Milo nodded. "Okay."

Bruce walked off in the opposite direction, and Milo

turned the corner with the cameraman close on his heels, only to see Harper and Austin making out in the hall. They didn't notice him right away, and the sight of his sister's mouth attached to some guy's wasn't something Milo could watch for very long. He cleared his throat, and the two broke apart quickly.

Austin's face paled, making the fading bruise from their first meeting stand out more than usual. Harper, on the other hand, stood up straighter and raised her brow in silent defiance, begging him to say something.

Milo hitched his thumb at the door. "Is Audrey inside?"

The corner of Harper's mouth twitched. "Yep. Why don't you go in, and I'll be there in a minute or two."

He took a deep breath. Harper was testing him, and Milo wasn't about to ruin things when they'd just begun mending their relationship. "Okay. I'll see you in a minute."

He looked Austin up and down. "That's *one* minute. Don't think I won't be watching the clock."

The cameraman chuckled behind Milo. He gave a light knock on the door, and when a faint "Come in," came from the other side, he hurried in to avoid the discomfort of catching Austin and Harper making out the second the door was closed.

"Milo!" Audrey squealed and ran over to him. She wrapped her arms around his waist, but when he tried to hug her back, she pulled away. "Careful, I can't mess my hair up right before the ceremony."

Milo stepped back and lifted his hands. "Okay. No hugs."

"You can hug me!" Sienna rushed over. "I'm

wearing my hair down so I don't have to worry about all that."

Milo hugged her tightly, so thankful to be near his family on this special day. When he finally let her go, and Sienna stepped back, his eyes inevitably went to Reagan.

Damn, Bruce was right.

She looked beautiful.

He opened his mouth to tell her that—and possibly much more—when there was a knock at the door.

It opened, and a crew member's head appeared. "Everyone ready?"

Milo looked at Audrey and gave her a wide smile. He tried not to let it falter when Reagan and Sienna walked into the hall to join Harper. He'd missed his chance, and time was running out.

"Don't worry," Audrey whispered in his ear. "There's always the dancing later. You can tell her then."

He turned with an open mouth to his sister. "How did you—"

She waved a hand. "I may not have seen you for ten years, but I know what a guy who's smitten looks like." She flushed. "You remind me of Eli when he looks at me."

"As happy as I am for you, I still don't think I'm totally comfortable hearing about the way my friend looks at my sister."

A corner of Audrey's mouth quirked up. "You might want to brace yourself then. I hear he might have to kiss me at the ceremony."

Milo forced his face into something solemn. "I'll try to prepare myself."

"Good, because there will be absolutely no more hitting from you. I think two black eyes is more than enough for one wedding." She punched his arm.

He chuckled and rubbed the spot she hit. "Okay. No more black eyes."

That was the only thing he could say with certainty. He still didn't know what he was going to do about the Reagan situation. He felt torn in two directions. The best thing to do was to give her space like Harper suggested. She'd just come out of a horrible relationship. He didn't want to take advantage of her broken heart.

But there was something growing between them. This thing was too special to let go just because the timing was terrible. It was small, and they both would need time to heal before they could jump into something romantic.

Would he be able to tell Reagan how he felt without scaring her off?

Would he be able to convince her, and himself, that they could take things slow?

Or would he have to let her go, and always remember Reagan as the one who got away?

Audrey stopped in the doorway and looked back at Milo. "You ready?"

He smiled at his sister. "As ready as I'll ever be."

TWENTY

The Day of the Dream Wedding

FOR ALL THE stress of the past week, the wedding ceremony was over before Reagan was even fully aware it had started.

She wished she could have taken a moment to soak it all in, but as terrible as she felt to admit it, she was glad it was over fast. Being in a wedding less than a day after your fiancé dumped you wasn't exactly easy.

It was about as easy as standing next to Milo as they waited for the wedding party to be announced at the reception. The entire time they stood there, Reagan was painfully aware of his presence. His familiar woodsy scent was impossible to escape, and when he held out his arm to her for their grand entrance into the barn filled with Audrey and Eli's wedding guests, all she could think about was the way he'd looked at her just before the girls left for the wedding ceremony.

That look had killed her—especially after she'd spent the previous evening thinking about Milo more than she should have, considering her recent breakup.

There had been an emotion Reagan wasn't willing

to name in Milo's expression, and she wasn't quite willing to admit how much being looked at that way felt right.

"How are you feeling?" Milo asked as they waited behind the rest of the wedding party. Reagan could hear the whooping and hollering from the other side of the closed barn door as Jason Castle did a little introduction.

"I'm fine." She looked down at her shoes, unable to look at Milo.

Soon, the doors to the barn opened, and Jason announced the bridesmaids and groomsmen in pairs. With a little creative shuffling, Fox ended up with Sienna, Wade escorted Harper, and Reagan was beside Milo. Walking into the barn on his arm felt so right.

"Are you sure you're okay?" Milo whispered when they took their places off to the side of the dance floor to await the newlyweds' arrival to start the party.

There were fewer cameras than the previous ten days. Now that the drama of the competitions was over, there wasn't much reason to film the actual wedding. Reagan knew that in shows like this, the wedding was only in the very last five minutes. The entire focus would be on the events leading up to it. Which could either be a good or a bad thing for Reagan.

"I'm fine," Reagan repeated. "Just wondering how much of my story with Harry will end up in the final cut for the show."

"I wouldn't worry about it too much." Milo gave her a lopsided smile that set her heart thudding in her chest. "There were quite a few other dramatic events that happened this week that Bruce may want to focus on instead."

"Like you punching Harry?" Reagan's lips quivered,

but instead of laughing, what came out of her mouth was halfway between a sob and a cough. Embarrassed, she turned away. "I'm sorry."

"Don't be." He reached out and put his hand on her arm. His touch was an anchor keeping her steady in the storm of emotions that threatened to take her away. She needed to keep it together for just a little longer for Audrey's sake.

"Ladies and gentlemen, please join me in welcoming the new Mr. and Mrs. Eli Flynn!"

Everyone in the barn cheered loudly. It was a small group of guests, nowhere near the several hundred Reagan would have had to host at a Woodly-Huntington wedding. Signing an image release had deterred quite a few of Audrey's friends and family, but those who were willing to be filmed were also willing to give the camera a show.

She looked so beautiful, but it was more than that. Audrey looked *happy*.

Reagan knew that was exactly how she wanted to look if she ever got married. She didn't want to be the perfect bride with every hair in place, and a dress that showed off all her best assets.

No, if Reagan ever took vows to spend the rest of her life with another person, she wanted to make sure she was smiling as brightly as Audrey was right now. That would be the most important thing. Not a false sense of security that came from marrying the "right kind of guy."

Harry breaking things off with her was the best thing that had ever happened to Reagan. The thought had come up over and over again as she spent some time alone the night before thinking about her relationship with Harry. Deep down, she knew that that truth had been there a lot longer. She just hadn't been able to see it.

Audrey and Eli walked out to the center of the dance floor, and the DJ started playing a slow song, chosen by the groomsmen, of course. Surprisingly, they'd done a really great job in choosing a song that was romantic without being over-the-top sappy.

"Let's get the rest of the wedding party, including the parents of the bride and groom out here for the next song," Jason said into the microphone as the song neared its end.

Reagan's breath caught in her chest as everyone shuffled out onto the dance floor.

Milo cleared his throat from beside her. "You don't have to if—"

"No, I'd like to dance. With you."

The corner of his mouth lifted, and he put out his hand for her to take. Reagan's fingers shook as she took it and followed him out to where the other couples were already swaying back and forth. Once they stopped, she took a deep breath and put her free hand on his shoulder. He put his hand on her waist, and she felt a jolt of electricity shoot through her at the contact.

She must have made a face because soon, Milo leaned in and whispered, "Is that okay?"

She didn't trust herself to speak, so she nodded.

They started moving slowly back and forth to the sweet slow melody.

"You look beautiful," Milo said.

Reagan felt her cheeks warm. "Thanks, Harry didn't like the dress, but I never got a chance to change it."

"The dress is pretty, but that's not what I meant."

KAYLA TIRRELL & DAPHNE JAMES HUFF

Milo shook his head. "I'm talking about you, Reagan. *You* look beautiful."

The breath she'd just managed to catch whooshed out of her. "Oh."

"I really wanted to tell you that when I first saw you with Audrey in the bride's room, but I didn't get the chance."

So *that* is what Milo had been thinking when he was looking at her. "Thank you. I think you look very handsome too."

He chuckled. "I wasn't giving you a compliment to get one in return."

"I know that." She really did. Milo's compliment was different from the begrudging ones she got from Harry. The ones that were somehow compliment and criticism, while expecting glowing praise in return. But it wasn't compulsion that led to her telling Milo he looked nice. He was incredibly handsome like he'd always been, and he was even better looking now than he'd been in college. He was just as sweet as he'd been then, too, but now she knew how strong and brave he was.

Before she realized what she was doing, Reagan rested her head on his chest and let the comforting sound of his steady heartbeat wash through her. He wrapped both of his arms around her and pulled her closer into the warm safety of his embrace. Much too soon for her liking, the song ended and something upbeat replaced it.

"Alright, alright." Jason's voice came through the speakers once again. "It's time to get this party started. Everyone get out here because we're about to celebrate!"

Milo pulled back and looked down at Reagan. "Do

you think we should…" He jerked his head toward the tables that were off to the side.

Reagan supposed they should move out of the way so people could start dancing, but she wasn't ready for this moment to end. In fact, she was pretty sure she could spend the rest of her life in Milo's arms.

She shook her head and leaned back against his chest. "No, I'm happy right here."

He held her like that through three more songs, and they danced slowly on the edge of the dance floor while the others flowed around them to the beat of the alt rock indie bands Fox and Wade had picked out. When Jason announced it was time to eat, Milo led Reagan outside without a word.

Hand in hand, they made their way down the lantern-lit path toward the chairs left over from the cere-mony. Milo gestured to a chair, but Reagan shook her head. If they sat, it would feel like a serious conversa-tion. And Reagan couldn't handle anything serious right now. So they kept walking, hand in hand.

Finally, Milo spoke. "I'm leaving tomorrow."

Reagan sucked in a breath. "I know."

"I'll be back as soon as I can. And I'd like to see you when I am." He looked at her and smiled. "Is that okay?"

She hesitated. It felt right, dancing in his arms, holding his hand. But she wasn't sure if she was ready for more.

"It doesn't have to mean anything," Milo said, when he saw her mouth turning down in a frown. "Whatever you want to do is fine with me."

Reagan's face suddenly split into a wide grin. It was three simple words, "whatever you want," but they were the exact right words she needed to hear right now. Harry had never said them, or when he did, it was out of obligation. She knew Milo meant them with all his heart.

With all her heart, she answered, "I want to see you when you come back."

Then she leaned in and kissed him under the star-filled sky on a warm summer evening in the mountains of North Carolina.

It was the end of something she was sad to let go of, but the beginning of something so much more.

Epilogue

THREE MONTHS AFTER THE DREAM WEDDING

"SHH. Quiet, everyone, it's going to start!" Audrey glared at the people in her living room, but a quick glance around made her smile too wide to hide behind an angry expression.

"We don't need to hear it. We know what happened; we were there." Sienna was perched on the arm of the couch, leaning against Fox. "I just want to know what I look like."

Harper playfully bumped her on her way to the armchair where Austin was sitting. "You'll look amazing, of course. Whereas, I know I'll look exhausted and stressed."

Austin rolled his eyes and reached up to take a mini wedding cake from the platter Harper carried.

Harper had insisted on having her chance at making a wedding cake for Audrey, and she'd outdone herself with perfect little miniature cakes—cakes, *not* cupcakes, Harper had specified. Each one had three layers of dark chocolate sponge, filled with white chocolate mousse, topped with an almond frosting.

"Isn't someone allergic to almonds?" Wade asked as he took a bite. He let out a small moan as he chewed. He was on his own tonight, but he'd been hinting at seeing someone. Audrey was dying for more details, but knew not to push.

"The person to whom you're referring was *not* invited to the viewing party." Audrey wrinkled her nose.

"What if the whole show is focused on him?" Fox frowned. "I mean, compared to what Sienna and I did, I think people would want that story more."

"Unless all his threats to sue actually went through," Eli said, coming into the room with a bottle of champagne. They'd been speculating about what footage would make the cut ever since the cameras had stopped rolling. Audrey hoped her best friend would be spared from seeing her breakup play out on TV, but Reagan insisted she didn't mind.

"It took going through that to get here," she'd said more than once in the past few months.

And "here" was pretty amazing for Reagan. Audrey had known her for over a decade, and never, in all of that time, had she ever looked so happy.

This week in particular had been a good one for her best friend. After weeks of waiting, Milo had finally moved back to Wellspring, with good news.

"Nobody talk about suing anybody, please." Milo groaned and picked up a cake for himself. "I've had enough of lawyers for a lifetime."

"I thought you'd change your mind after what yours did for you." Reagan came up beside him and snuck a bite of his cake before it was even halfway to his mouth.

"True," he said. "They brought me back home sooner than I ever imagined." He planted a kiss on top of her head. "Back to you."

Reagan flushed. Milo had returned to Australia the day after the wedding expecting to stay for months while his divorce finalized, but he'd had a happy surprise waiting for him. His ex had fallen in love and wanted to get married right away, so Milo's lawyers had used that to their advantage, and she'd agreed to all the terms, including giving him half the proceeds from the sale of their house.

He wasn't rich, but he'd be able to go back to school and finish his degree. Audrey couldn't tell who was happier about how things had turned out—the Hudson girls or her best friend. One look at Reagan's face, however, and she knew the answer.

"Okay, everyone, that's enough." Audrey turned up the volume on the TV. "It's starting."

As she settled in on the couch next to her husband— it still gave her a thrill to think of him that way—and her family, she wondered who would be next to have their own dream wedding.

Hers hadn't gone exactly the way she'd planned, but it had brought her sisters happiness and her brother back home. They'd all been the lucky winners of *Wedding Games*.

Acknowledgments

Daphne and Kayla would like to thank their husbands for putting up with their crazy, and their kids for being so darn adorable.

Thank you to Designed with Grace for this amazing cover.

Thank you to EditElle for proofreading this book.

And to our AMAZING readers, thank you for letting us keep this dream alive.

About the Authors

Daphne and Kayla have been writing buddies since 2017.

They have three joint series together, but this is their first cowriting project.

Between the two of them they have: four kids, three cats, two husbands, and one fierce love of writing.

Kayla wishes she could eat tacos every day, and Daphne will never turn down free cake.

You can find them online at:

www.daphnejameshuff.com

www.tirrellblewrites.com

CPSIA information can be obtained
at www.ICGtesting.com
Printed in the USA
LVHW101603301022
731926LV00005B/137